It was hopel[...]

She stared acro[...]
suddenly lean back in his seat with a strangely
rueful smile.

'I should have warned you, Sister. Amongst all
my other faults, I'm afraid I also have no
conversation.'

'I'd noticed,' Izzie replied without thinking,
only to flush scarlet.

She was insulting him all over again, but as
she gazed at him, conscience-stricken, his
smile actually widened.

'Do you always say exactly what you think?'
he asked.

'If you mean am I usually quite so tactless,
then the answer's no.' She sighed.

'So, it's only me who brings out the honesty
in you?'

Maggie Kingsley lives with her family in a remote cottage in the north of Scotland surrounded by sheep and deer. She is from a family with a strong medical tradition, and has enjoyed a varied career including lecturing and working for a major charity, but writing has always been her first love. When not writing, she combines working for an employment agency with her other interest, interior design.

Recent titles by the same author:

A BABY TO LOVE
PARTNERS IN LOVE
DANIEL'S DILEMMA

IZZIE'S CHOICE

BY
MAGGIE KINGSLEY

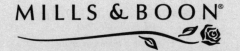
MILLS & BOON®

First published in Great Britain 1999
Harlequin Mills & Boon Limited,
Eton House, 18-24 Paradise Road, Richmond, Surrey TW9 1SR

© Maggie Kingsley 1999

ISBN 0 263 81763 6

Set in Times Roman 10½ on 11¼ pt.
03-9908-53829-D

Printed and bound in Spain
by Litografia Rosés S.A., Barcelona

CHAPTER ONE

'I MEAN it, Izzie, the man's a real pain,' Steve declared as he stretched past her into the bathroom cabinet. 'He's arrogant, domineering—'

'It can't be easy for Mr Farrell—starting a new job, moving from Newcastle to Kelso,' she observed, ducking under his arm to retrieve her hairbrush. 'Maybe he just hasn't found his feet yet.'

'Oh, he's found them all right,' Steve replied, his blue eyes stormy as he took his aftershave out of the bathroom cabinet and banged the door shut. 'He's been using his size twelves to walk over everybody in A and E for the last two weeks.'

It certainly didn't sound encouraging, Izzie decided as she struggled to subdue her long corn-coloured curls into a neat topknot. When Charlie Wright had been Kelso General's A and E consultant it had been a happy, close-knit department, but Charlie had moved to a job down south and now it seemed that everything had changed—and not for the better.

'Perhaps he just needs more time to settle in,' she suggested through a mouthful of hairclips. 'Perhaps if you talked to him—'

'*Talked* to him?' Steve exclaimed. 'Sweetie, Ben Farrell doesn't talk. He orders and we obey—it's as simple as that.'

A deep frown creased Izzie's forehead. In the six months since Steve had joined A and E as Senior House Officer, and the three months he'd been living with her, she'd never once seen him angry, but this morning...

'I wish I'd been here when he arrived,' she murmured. 'If I'd been here instead of on holiday—'

'It wouldn't have made a damn bit of difference, believe me,' Steve interrupted. 'Nobody—but nobody—could get through to Ben Farrell.'

Maybe not, she thought, but if this Ben Farrell was as stuffy as Steve suggested, he could have mistaken Steve's laid-back attitude to life for a lack of commitment and she could at least have set him straight on that.

'Steve, about Mr Farrell—'

'Do you have to keep on talking about him?' he snapped. 'The man's a jerk—OK?'

She followed him out of the bathroom, her brown eyes troubled. She hadn't been the one who'd done nothing but talk about their new boss since they'd got up this morning, but something told her it might not be wise to point that out.

'I still don't see why you've got to move back into staff accommodation,' she said instead as he put his aftershave into his suitcase. 'Your exams aren't until the end of August—'

'Izzie, these exams are important to me,' he flared. 'Do you think I want to stay a senior house officer all my life?'

She understood—of course she did—but, try as she may, she couldn't hide her disappointment and, seeing it, he raked his hands through his blond hair and reached for her.

'I'm sorry, sweetheart. I shouldn't be yelling at you—it isn't right, and it isn't fair. How are your folks? I forgot to ask about them when you got back last night.'

She arched against him and chuckled as she remembered only too clearly what had been uppermost in his mind last night. 'My dad's OK, but my mother's angina's been troubling her—'

'Hell, is that the time?' he interrupted, abruptly releasing her. 'I'd better get my skates on. Our new boss likes us to be in at least half an hour before our shift starts so he can update us on any problems before we clock on.'

'Oh, Steve, why didn't you tell me?' she protested in

consternation. 'It's already a quarter past seven—I'm never going to make it by half past!'

'Relax, Sister Clark.' He grinned as she began scrambling into her clothes. 'Mr Personality won't expect you to know the new rule—you've been on holiday, remember?'

'Yes, but—'

'It's really great to have you back,' he declared, leaning forward to kiss her lightly on the nose. 'I've missed you.'

'And I've missed you,' she answered, but she doubted whether he'd heard her. He was already striding out the door, and she sped across to the window to catch a last brief glimpse of him getting into his car.

He was so handsome, she thought with a deep sigh—handsome, and charming, and fun—and yet he'd fallen in love with her. A girl who had nothing to commend her but a pair of laughing brown eyes and a mass of ungovernable corn-coloured curls. A girl who at five feet eleven was as tall as he was.

And he did love her. OK, so he hadn't actually asked her to marry him yet but, as she'd told her mother, it was only a matter of time, and when you'd fallen head over heels in love with someone like Steve Melville you knew better than to push for a definite date.

She sighed again as she watched him drive away. The next six weeks were going to seem like a lifetime but, as he'd said, these exams were important to him and it wasn't fair of her to grumble. At least she'd be able to see him at work every day but her flat was going to be so empty, so lonely, without him.

Slowly she turned from the window then let out a shriek when she saw the time. If she didn't get a move on she wouldn't even arrive at the Kelso General for eight o'clock, and if Steve's description of Ben Farrell was anything to go by the new A and E consultant would hang her out to dry.

*   *   *

'Good holiday?' Fran Walton smiled, when Izzie dashed breathlessly into A and E's small staffroom at exactly twenty to eight.

'Lovely, thanks,' she answered, pulling off her jacket and hanging it quickly up behind the door. For a second she studied the brown fabric indecisively and then made up her mind. 'Fran, what's this Mr Farrell really like?'

'Really like?' the staff nurse echoed in surprise.

'In appearance, I mean,' Izzie said quickly, though in truth she was not one bit interested in their new boss's looks.

Fran pushed her spectacles further up her nose and frowned. 'Well, he's got black hair and grey eyes—'

'And he's quite old if you're talking about who I think you're talking about,' Tess Golding chipped in as she bounced into the staffroom. 'In fact, his hair's going grey at the sides.'

'Lots of people go grey early, young lady,' Fran snapped. 'And Mr Farrell's not old. He's only forty.'

The student nurse and Izzie exchanged veiled glances. It was common knowledge that Fran would reach the big four-O next year and just as common knowledge that she was acutely sensitive about it.

'Short, tall, good-looking, ordinary?' Izzie asked swiftly, deciding that it might be wise to move the conversation away from the thorny question of age.

'Tall,' Tess said positively. 'I get a crick in my neck every time I talk to him.'

'You get a crick in your neck when you're talking to some of the ten-year-olds who come into A and E,' Fran said with a chuckle, and Tess stuck out her tongue at her.

'OK, OK, so I'm a midget, but he really is tall. As to whether he's good-looking…' She wrinkled her nose. 'I wouldn't say so, would you, Staff?'

Fran shook her head and Izzie cleared her throat awkwardly. 'Steve…Steve seems to feel he's a bit…well, a bit domineering.'

To her surprise Fran looked decidedly uncomfortable, and it was Tess who answered.

'He's certainly got very definite ideas about how things should be done, but as long as you do what he says he's OK. And you know what Steve's like,' Tess continued, seeing Izzie frown. 'Always laughing, always joking, and Mr Farrell's got no sense of humour.'

'What—none at all?' Izzie exclaimed in surprise.

Tess shook her head.

'The only thing that interests him is work,' Fran declared. 'And speaking of which,' she continued as she got to her feet, 'we'd better get ourselves out on duty fast. Lack of punctuality really gets up his nose.'

Never had Izzie seen the staffroom empty so fast. When Charlie had been in charge everything had been a lot more casual, a lot more laid-back, and instinctively she went across to the mirror to check her appearance.

Her deep blue sister's uniform was immaculate, her sensible black shoes gleamed with much polishing—only her wayward hair let her down, as usual. With a muttered oath she dived into her handbag and ruthlessly set about pinning back the recalcitrant curls that had somehow managed to work themselves free from under her cap.

It was a pointless task, and she knew it. Within half an hour more curls would undoubtedly have made their escape but at least she looked reasonably neat now, she decided as she stared critically at her reflection. Whether she did, or whether she didn't, however, she knew she'd have to get a move on, and with a sigh she rammed her cap further down onto her head, opened the staffroom door and cannoned straight into a white-coated stranger.

'S-sorry,' she stammered, as two large hands reached out to steady her. Two large hands that belonged to a man with thick black hair that was greying at the temples. A quick glance at his name-tag confirmed his identity and her lips curved into a smile of welcome. 'Good morning, Mr Farrell. I'm Sister Izzie Clark—'

'And you're late.'

The smile on her face died. Well, so much for the ordinary pleasantries of life like 'Hello' and 'It's nice to meet you', she thought.

Pointedly she lifted the small watch pinned to her uniform. 'I'm not late, Mr Farrell. I don't go on duty until eight, and it's only two minutes to—'

'And I specifically requested that all A and E staff should be in the department at least half an hour before their shift starts,' he interrupted tersely.

'So I understand,' she replied, her voice equally cool. 'But I've been on holiday and I only learned about the new rule forty-five minutes ago.'

He stared down at her, his grey eyes totally unreadable, and to her surprise she found that she actually had to tilt her head to meet his gaze.

Tess had been wrong. Ben Farrell wasn't just tall, he was huge. Six feet four at a conservative estimate, and every inch of it was solid muscle. I could actually wear high heels if I went out with this man, Izzie thought with a surge of delight, only to immediately shake her head. Now, where in the world had that ridiculous idea come from?

A deep frown suddenly appeared in his grey eyes. 'What kind of name is that—Izzie?'

Her smile returned. 'I was actually christened Isabella, but one of my brothers couldn't pronounce it when he was little so he called me Izzie instead and the name's sort of stuck.'

'Has it?' he said drily, and to her annoyance she felt her cheeks redden.

It had never occurred to her before that it might be considered silly to retain her childhood name, but somehow this man had just made it seem so.

'Mr Farrell—'

'In future I'd be obliged if you'd attempt to be on time, Sister,' he interrupted. 'It sets a very bad example to the rest of the nursing staff if someone of your seniority doesn't obey the rules.'

She gazed after him, open-mouthed, as he strode away from her. Well, *really*! Anyone would think that she'd deliberately set out to flout his stupid new rule. How on earth was she expected to know about it? She wasn't a mind-reader.

Quickly she hurried after him through the swing doors into Reception, fully intending to give him a piece of her mind, but she didn't get the chance. He was already deep in conversation with their receptionist.

'It's mostly just the walking wounded today, Mr Farrell,' she heard April declare. 'A couple of sprains, someone with a splinter in their finger—'

'A what?' he demanded as he lifted the logbook from the counter.

'I know, I know.' April sighed. 'This is an A and E unit, but trying to get that into some people's skulls is like drilling for oil. There's a Mrs Bolton in cubicle 3—severe abdominal pains—a Mrs Taylor in cubicle 2 with a badly cut right hand—'

'And the little old lady sitting by the window?' he queried as his gaze swept over Reception. 'What's wrong with her?'

April's eyes met Izzie's in panic-stricken appeal and deftly she whisked the logbook out of Mr Farrell's fingers.

'Nothing serious,' she said smoothly. 'I understand Dr Melville will be seeing her shortly.'

For a second she thought he was going to argue, then he nodded. 'OK, Sister. Let's take a look at Mrs Bolton.'

Obediently Izzie followed him through to the treatment area but she knew she'd merely postponed the inevitable.

Ben Farrell was bound to find out eventually that there

was never anything wrong with Mavis. The little old lady just liked sitting in Reception, chatting to the waiting casualties, and once Charlie had established she was harmless he hadn't minded her constant presence. Privately Izzie suspected that Mavis was simply lonely but she very much doubted whether Ben Farrell would accept that as a valid reason for her continual appearance in A and E.

'I understand you're experiencing abdominal pains, Mrs Bolton?' Ben declared as he pulled back the curtains around cubicle 3 to reveal a white-faced, middle-aged woman lying on the trolley.

'I thought it was something I'd eaten last night, Doctor,' she replied, her bottom lip trembling, 'but the pain's gradually been getting worse and worse—'

'And is it a stabbing or a grumbling pain?' he interrupted.

'A bit of both, really,' she answered, wincing. 'I'm sorry I can't be a bit more specific. All I do know is that it's bloody painful— Sorry, Nurse.'

'No need to apologise.' Izzie chuckled as she unbuttoned the woman's blouse and loosened her skirt. 'I've heard a lot worse in my time, believe me.'

'Does this hurt?' Ben Farrell asked as he gently began pressing Mrs Bolton's stomach with his fingertips. 'Or how about—?'

'There!' she yelled, doubling up as he touched the right-hand side of her stomach. 'It hurts there, and I'm sorry but…I think…I think I'm going to be sick!'

Izzie got a bowl under her chin just in time.

'It looks very much as though it's your appendix, Mrs Bolton,' Ben Farrell said when she eventually subsided back onto her pillow. 'I'll make arrangements for you to be admitted—'

'You mean, I'll have to stay?' she interrupted, whitening still further. 'But my husband…my family… I didn't even tell them I was coming here this morning in case all I had was an upset stomach.'

'Our receptionist will contact your family and let them know what's happening.'

'But—'

'The pain isn't going to go away, Mrs Bolton,' Ben interrupted gently. 'In fact, it could get a lot worse.'

'Yes, but—'

'No buts, Mrs Bolton,' he broke in, his voice suddenly stern. 'You're here, and here you're going to stay.'

'Heavens, but he's masterful when he's roused, isn't he, Nurse?' Mrs Bolton declared with a wobbly laugh, and Izzie saw a ghost of a smile appear on Ben Farrell's dark face.

Tess had been right when she'd said he wasn't handsome. His features were too harsh and his expression was too forbidding, but he had a strong face, a striking face, a face you'd always remember. Tess had also said that he had no sense of humour and yet there were laughter lines around his eyes and mouth. There were also deep frown lines on his forehead and she couldn't help but wonder what—or who—had put them there.

'I'm sorry to disturb you, Sister,' he said suddenly, 'but if you could possibly come down out of the clouds for a minute would you ask Nurse Golding to make Mrs Bolton more comfortable while I phone Women's Surgical?'

Izzie's cheeks were scarlet as he swept past her. What on earth had got into her—letting her mind wander like that? Talk about behaving unprofessionally…

'I expect he just got out of bed on the wrong side this morning, Nurse,' Mrs Bolton observed, gazing up at her sympathetically.

Izzie had a horrible suspicion that Ben Farrell never got out of bed on the right side but she managed to nod, before stepping through the curtains and closing them behind her.

Of all the stupid things she could have done, letting her

mind wander definitely had to be the worst. Ben Farrell must think she was the most incompetent nurse he'd ever met. Well, she'd show him, she told herself. She'd be so damned efficient from now on he'd be forced to revise his opinion of her.

That, at least, was her plan but as the day wore on she came to the depressing conclusion that, far from acknowledging she was good at her job, Ben Farrell was clearly harbouring grave doubts about her ability to do it at all.

He never took his eyes off her for a minute. She only had to start explaining some procedure to Tess and he was there, listening. Every time she dressed a wound or fitted a drip, she'd look up and find him watching. By half past five her nerves were in shreds and her temper was paper-thin.

'Are you OK?' Steve asked with concern when she'd walked past him for the second time in ten minutes without saying a word.

'No, I'm not OK,' she muttered as she consulted the whiteboard on which the names of the patients who were being treated was written.

He studied her for a minute and then a wry smile appeared on his lips. 'Ben Farrell?'

'Got it in one,' she exclaimed. 'Honestly, Steve, that man—'

'Sister Clark!'

She closed her eyes. Never had she thought she could be sick to death of hearing the sound of her own name, but she was sick to death of hearing it coming out of Ben Farrell's mouth today. And the words 'please' and 'thank you' didn't appear to exist in his vocabulary.

With an effort she straightened her shoulders and walked down the treatment room towards him.

'I've a two-year-old in here with sudden, unexplained deafness,' he declared. 'According to his mother, he's a little uncomfortable but not in any great pain.'

The child's mother was right. Little Fraser Reynolds appeared totally unconcerned by his sudden deafness but Mrs Reynolds was perilously close to tears.

'He seemed perfectly fine last night, Doctor,' she declared tremulously. 'He was a bit quiet when I put him to bed but we'd been on a picnic so I thought he was just tired. And then today… Every time I've spoken to him he just doesn't seem to hear me.'

'Have you noticed him shaking his head at all, Mrs… Mrs…?'

'Reynolds,' Izzie murmured tactfully.

A brusque nod in her direction was Ben Farrell's only indication that he had heard.

'Yes, he has,' Mrs Reynolds replied. 'Is…is that bad?'

'Not necessarily,' he answered, taking his auriscope out of his pocket. 'Sister, could you hold the child's head steady for me?'

Quickly Izzie did as he'd asked.

'Can you see anything?' Mrs Reynolds whispered as Ben squinted through the auriscope into her son's ears.

'I can see something.' He frowned. 'And it looks like…a bead, a green bead.'

'A bead?' Mrs Reynolds repeated.

'You wouldn't believe the things that children can inhale, swallow or stick in their ears,' Ben declared as he straightened up. 'Peanuts, coins, marbles, buttons—I once had a child who swallowed a battery.'

'But I don't have any green necklaces,' Mrs Reynolds protested.

'Well, he seems to have got hold of one from somewhere,' he observed. 'Sister Clark, could you get me—?'

'Forceps and a syringe,' she completed for him smoothly. 'I won't be a minute, Mr Farrell.'

She didn't even wait to see his expression. She simply strode out of the cubicle and returned seconds later with the equipment.

'OK, if you could hold him for me again, Sister,' he murmured as Fraser gazed up at him, his large blue eyes suddenly distinctly wary. 'And be prepared for any sudden movements. The last thing I want is for him to jerk away from me.'

An angry retort sprang to her lips and she crushed it down quickly. She wasn't a novice. She was twenty-six years old and a fully trained sister. She knew as well as he did that he could inflict serious damage on the child's ear canal if he wasn't careful, but she gritted her teeth and managed to smile down at Fraser.

'Mr Farrell wants to take another little look inside your ear,' she said softly. 'It might feel a little bit ticklish to start with,' she added, tightening her grip slightly as Ben deftly inserted the forceps into Fraser's ear and the child began to squirm, 'but it will soon be over, and then—'

'Got it,' Ben interrupted with satisfaction. 'And it's not a bead,' he added as he held the tiny forceps up to the light. 'It's a pea—a half-defrosted pea.'

'How in the world did he get hold of that?' Mrs Reynolds said in confusion. 'And more to the point—why on earth would he want to stick it in his ear?'

'The "how" is easy,' Ben declared. 'You must have dropped it on the floor when you were preparing dinner last night. As to the "why"—I'm afraid children will stick practically anything in their ears or up their noses, just for the hell of it. If you want my advice, stick to carrots in future—they're a lot more visible.'

To Izzie's surprise he was actually smiling, and it made him look so much more human that she instinctively smiled back, only to see all trace of amusement immediately disappear from his face.

What the hell was wrong with him? she wondered as he strode through the curtains without a word. It was only a smile, and yet anyone would think she'd just done something completely outrageous.

'I feel such a fool,' Mrs Reynolds declared as she lifted her son into her arms. 'If I'd known what it was, I could probably have got it out myself.'

'You must never try to take something out of someone's ear,' Izzie said quickly. 'Unless you're experienced, you could actually push it further in and cause more damage. Always get medical help.'

'Well, I'm very grateful to you, Nurse,' Mrs Reynolds said warmly as Izzie accompanied her out into the reception area. 'And please thank the doctor for me—he's nice, isn't he?'

Nice? Izzie thought acidly as she managed a weak smile in reply. He wasn't nice—he wasn't nice at all.

But he's good at his job, a little voice whispered in the back of her mind. Oh, yes, he's good, she argued back, but a machine would have been just as good, and who wanted to work for a machine?

With a sigh she turned to go back into the treatment room and came to a halt. There was a girl sitting in Reception— a girl with stunning red hair and large green eyes. Somewhere in the back of her mind a memory stirred and she took a step forward uncertainly.

'Joanna?' she ventured. 'Joanna Ogilvy?'

The girl turned, clearly puzzled, and then a wave of recognition lit up her face. 'Izzie—Izzie Clark! My God, I haven't seen you since...since...'

'Mrs Benson's A Level biology classes at Kelso High School eight years ago,' Izzie chuckled.

'That's right,' Joanna exclaimed in amazement. 'You were determined to go into nursing—'

'And you were equally determined to marry Brian Morrison.'

'I did, too, and divorced him four years later.' Joanna laughed. 'What about you? Are you married or engaged or anything?'

'I'm not married or engaged, but I'm definitely working on the "anything",' Izzie replied, her brown eyes dancing.

Joanna shook her head. 'You haven't changed a bit.'

'If you mean I haven't got any shorter then you're absolutely right.' Izzie smiled. 'What are you doing here? The last I heard, you'd moved to Edinburgh—'

'Sister Clark.'

Her heart sank. Couldn't she even exchange a few words with an old friend without Ben Farrell spying on her? The clock on the reception wall indicated that her shift was over. She was on her own time now and what she did, and who she talked to, were her own affair.

'Something I can do for you, Mr Farrell?' she asked, turning towards him, her face cool.

'I just wondered if there was a problem,' he declared, glancing from her to Joanna. 'I saw you leaving the treatment room with Mrs Reynolds but you seemed to have been gone rather a long time.'

In other words, he suspected she might be slacking, she thought with mounting fury.

'I ran into an old friend,' she said stiffly. 'Joanna, this is Mr Farrell, our head of department. Mr Farrell—Joanna Ogilvy.'

'You're not ill, I hope, Mrs Ogilvy?' he asked.

'It's "Miss", actually,' she replied, fluttering her long, dark eyelashes at him and flashing him a brilliant smile. 'I'm here with my father. He put a nail through his thumb when he was doing some DIY.'

'Ah—the gentleman in cubicle 2.' He nodded. 'One of our nurses is dressing his hand so he shouldn't be much longer.'

'Oh, I don't mind waiting,' she murmured dulcetly. 'In fact, I think I could quite happily wait here all night.'

A slight nod from Ben was Joanna's only answer and as he walked away she let out a low appreciative whistle. 'Is he the "anything" you're working on, Izzie?'

'You must be joking!' she gasped.

'Anything but,' Joanna declared, running a beautifully manicured hand through her short red curls. 'I just adore these strong, dark, brooding types who look as though they've had an unhappy past, don't you?'

'No, I don't,' Izzie said firmly. 'Look, it's been really nice seeing you again,' she continued quickly as the girl opened her mouth, clearly intending to continue the conversation, 'but I'm afraid I've got to go. How long are you staying in Kelso?'

'I was planning to go back to Edinburgh at the end of the week,' Joanna declared with a thoughtful smile, 'but I think I might stick around a little while longer. The countryside's suddenly become a whole lot more attractive.'

Izzie shook her head as she left Reception. Strong, dark brooding types with an unhappy past—what a load of old baloney! She'd bet money that Ben Farrell's past consisted solely of making other people miserable.

And it looked as though he was continuing his life's work, she thought as she caught sight of him, talking to Steve. One look at Steve's disgruntled expression said it all.

'What is it?' she asked as soon as Steve was alone. 'What's wrong?'

'I'm sick to death of being treated like some first-year medical student,' Steve retorted. 'I know I should have erased Mr Maxwell's name from the board when he was discharged, but I had a patient bleeding like a stuck pig in 4 and in my opinion it was more important to treat him.'

'Steve—'

'I don't have to put up with this, Izzie,' he interrupted, his handsome face furious. 'I could get an SHO post anywhere!'

She bit her lip as he banged out of the treatment room. That was all she needed—Steve threatening to resign. OK, so he really should have taken Mr Maxwell's name off the

board immediately, and it wouldn't have taken him a second to do it, but the thought of him leaving the Kelso
General…maybe leaving her…

Quickly she hurried after him and found him in the staffroom.

'Look, I know you're upset,' she declared as he threw
his white coat angrily into the laundry basket, 'but can't
you simply ignore him?'

'How?' he demanded. 'How can you ignore someone
who tells you you're too casual, too friendly, and that one
day, if you're not careful, it might have disastrous consequences on your work!'

She blinked. 'He said that?'

Steve nodded and furious anger surged within her.

'Well, one thing's for sure,' she exclaimed. 'His work is
never going to suffer because I very much doubt if he's got
any friends!'

'Izzie—'

'Of all the pompous…arrogant… He's nothing but a big
bully, Steve.'

'Izzie—'

'And he's not just a bully,' she continued, her brown
eyes stormy. 'He's a prat as well. Hanging around everyone
like a bad smell—snooping and criticising like he's God's
gift to medicine. I feel sorry for him, I really do. There
must be something sadly lacking in his life if the only way
he can get his kicks is—'

'*Izzie!*'

'What? What is it?' she demanded angrily.

And suddenly she knew. Steve was looking at her with
such clear embarrassment that she knew she was going to
find herself gazing up into Ben Farrell's cool grey eyes
when she turned round.

'M-Mr Farrell,' she stammered, hot colour flooding her
cheeks. 'I didn't… I mean I wasn't—'

'Could I have a word with you, Sister?' he interrupted.

She followed him out into the corridor with dragging steps. She was in deep trouble, and she knew it. No matter what her private opinions might be, this man was her boss, and if he chose he could make life downright impossible for her. It was time for some mega-grovelling and she opened her mouth to do just that when he forestalled her.

'I clearly owe you an apology, don't I?'

Her jaw dropped. '*You?* But you haven't done anything—'

'I must have done something to give you such a very poor opinion of me,' he interrupted ruefully. 'I've been watching you all day, Sister, and you're clearly a very fine nurse. I'd thought... I'd hoped that we could work well together.'

She couldn't say a word. She couldn't even meet his eyes. She just stared at his crisp white shirt and elegant green tie, and wished the ground would open up and swallow her.

'I know I have a sharp tongue,' he continued. 'I'm not proud of it, and it's something I've been trying to correct.' He paused and cleared his throat. 'Clearly I haven't succeeded, but please believe me when I saw that if I've hurt you today, or upset you, then I'm truly, deeply sorry.'

The colour on her cheeks darkened to crimson. She had to say something—she knew she had—and she forced herself to look up at him, only to see such clear concern on his face that she found she couldn't say anything at all.

'I've been called a great many things in my time, Sister,' he observed, with an oddly twisted smile, 'but this is the first time I've ever been called a prat. I promise I'll do my very best not to appear one in future.'

He began to walk away from her and at last she found her voice. 'Mr Farrell, wait—come back!'

But he didn't come back. He just kept on walking until he disappeared through the door at the end of the corridor.

'What did he say?' Steve asked as he came cautiously out of the staffroom. 'Did he tear a strip off you?'

She bit her lip. 'No...no, he didn't.'

'You mean, you actually managed to silence that big windbag?' he said in amazement. 'Ye gods, if I'd known it was as easy as that I'd have given him an earful myself.'

She shook her head uncomfortably. 'I wish he hadn't heard what I said, Steve.'

'Rubbish!' he exclaimed. 'It's high time Mr High-and-Mighty Farrell was taken down a peg or two. I'm proud of you, kid.'

But Izzie didn't feel proud of herself. She felt like a worm—lower than a worm.

Steve might say that Ben Farrell had got what he deserved but she wasn't at all sure now that he had. He could have torn her character to shreds—and she wouldn't have blamed him if he had—but he hadn't even looked angry when he'd been talking to her. He'd looked hurt. The man she'd considered a cold, unemotional machine had looked hurt, and she found herself wishing with all her heart that she'd kept her big mouth shut.

CHAPTER TWO

A FROWN appeared on Izzie's forehead as she scanned the hospital canteen, looking for an empty seat. To her dismay it looked as though the entire hospital staff had decided to take their lunch break at the same time.

'Izzie—Izzie, over here!'

Her frown cleared as she saw Steve waving to her and quickly she started towards him only to pause. Ben Farrell was sitting by himself at a table near the window and he looked…lonely. OK, so he'd piled a stack of books on the empty seat beside him, which didn't exactly suggest that he wanted company and yet…

Admit it, Izzie, she told herself as she stared across at him. You feel guilty. He's scarcely said a word to you all week, and you feel guilty as hell.

For a second she hesitated and then, before she could change her mind, she eased her way through the tables towards him, all too conscious that Steve was staring after her in amazement.

If Steve was surprised by her action, however, Mr Farrell looked totally confounded.

'Something I can do for you, Sister?' he asked with a slight frown when she appeared beside him.

A smile would do for a start, she thought, but she didn't say that.

'Do you mind if I join you?' she said instead.

For a moment the frown in his eyes deepened, then he lifted the books from the seat opposite him and put them on the floor.

So far, so good, she thought as she put her plate of soup on the table and sat down. Now make conversation, Izzie, she told herself as she picked up her spoon. The secret to any good working relationship is conversation.

'You must be finding working in Kelso quite a change from Newcastle, Mr Farrell,' she observed.

He pushed his scarcely touched meal away from him. 'It's a lot smaller, certainly.'

'But you're enjoying it?' she pressed. 'I mean, you don't regret the move?'

He shrugged. 'I think one hospital is pretty much the same as any other, really.'

'The Kelso General isn't,' she observed. 'It's truly part of the community. When we have our annual August fair virtually everyone in the area turns up to support us.'

'Do they?'

Total lack of interest was plain in his voice as she grimly spooned some soup into her mouth. Talk about an uphill struggle. Getting this man to make any kind of conversation was like drawing teeth, but she'd never been the kind of girl who gave up easily.

'But surely you must have thought the Kelso General was different,' she declared determinedly, 'or why choose to come here at all?'

'I like fishing, and the Tweed is one of the best salmon rivers in the country.'

She couldn't help but laugh. 'It is but, seriously—what made you decide to come to Kelso?'

'I told you—I like fishing.'

It was hopeless, she decided as she stared across at him, absolutely hopeless, only to see him suddenly lean back in his seat with a strangely rueful smile.

'I should have warned you, Sister. Amongst all my other faults, I'm afraid I also have no conversation.'

'I'd noticed,' she replied without thinking, only to flush scarlet.

What on earth had made her say that? She was insulting

him all over again, but as she gazed at him, conscience-stricken, his smile actually widened.

'Do you always say exactly what you think?' he asked.

'If you mean am I usually quite so tactless, then the answer's no.' She sighed.

'So, it's only me who brings out the honesty in you?'

'Yes… I mean no… I mean… Oh, heck.' She laughed. 'Can I have more time to think about that before I answer?'

He chuckled, a low, deep sound that was strangely attractive, and to her annoyance she found herself blushing.

'I seem to be forever saying the wrong thing to you, don't I?' she observed. 'Which reminds me, I never did apologise—'

He waved a hand at her dismissively. 'Forget it.'

'But—'

'I said forget it,' he said firmly. 'It's in the past and best forgotten.'

He meant it. She could see that he did and, encouraged, she cleared her throat. 'At the risk of offending you again, can I give you a little bit of advice?'

'That sounds ominous,' he observed. 'OK—fire away.'

'You'd get an awful lot more out of people if you weren't so brusque. Tess is really keen, even though she's still a student, and Fran—there's nothing she doesn't know about A and E. And Steve—'

'What about Steve?'

Something about his tone told her she should stop right there but, having started, she felt compelled to finish.

'Do you have to be so hard on him?' she said quickly. 'I know he occasionally appears a bit…well, maybe a bit slapdash, but he's a good doctor, and it doesn't help if you criticise him all the time.'

His lip curled. 'I wasn't aware I did, or that Dr Melville was such a sensitive soul.'

She opened her mouth, then closed it again. She should never have started this conversation. Not only had she made

Steve look like a whinging wimp, but she also had the very distinct impression that she'd suddenly gone down in his estimation. Quite why that should bother her she didn't know, but it did.

'Mr Farrell—'

'I understand that you and Steve Melville are…an item?'

'That's right,' she replied, annoyingly aware that she was blushing again under his steady gaze.

'So you'll be getting married soon?'

'I don't know… I mean, I expect we will eventually,' she added swiftly as his eyebrows rose. 'We're not actually engaged or anything, but we are committed to one another.'

'I see.'

She didn't think he did. 'The thing is, we've both got too much on our plates at the moment to set a wedding date,' she continued hurriedly. 'Steve wants to move up to specialist registrar, and that involves a lot of studying, and I…well, I'm really busy, too, and…and we're happy as we are.'

'I'm delighted to hear it.'

She gazed at him impotently. Why had she felt the need to defend both Steve and herself? She didn't need to—there was nothing to defend. They'd been happy living together, and if they hadn't set a wedding date yet it had nothing to do with Ben Farrell. Not that he'd actually suggested that it did, she remembered. In fact, he really hadn't said anything at all so why did she feel uncomfortable, defensive?

To her relief his pager sounded and as he eased himself up from his seat she got to her feet, too.

'There's no need for you to come,' he said. 'Stay and finish your soup.'

She gulped down the remnants quickly and smiled up at him, her eyes watering. 'It's finished.'

He shook his head. 'You're going to end up with ulcers.'

'No chance.' She grinned. 'Cast-iron stomach, that's me.'

To her surprise he actually laughed, and as she followed him out of the canteen a slight frown creased her forehead.

Steve had been wrong. Ben Farrell might be a bit brusque, and she most definitely wouldn't want to make an enemy of him, but when he smiled he was really rather likeable. Not that she could ever become interested in him herself, of course—the very idea was too ridiculous for words—but he most certainly wasn't the stiff-necked martinet Steve had accused him of being.

'What's the problem, Staff?' Ben asked as they strode into the treatment room to find Fran waiting for them.

'A Mr Martin Kent with an eye injury. Apparently he was making a bookcase for his wife's birthday and suddenly felt a sharp pain in his right eye.'

Ben nodded and pulled back the curtains around cubicle 3.

'I understand you've had a bit of an accident, Mr Kent?' he observed, gazing down at the young man sitting on the end of the trolley squinting awkwardly up at him.

'It's probably nothing, Doctor—'

'I think you should let me be the best judge of that,' Ben interrupted, taking his ophthalmoscope out of his pocket. 'Could you look over my shoulder for me? That's right—keep looking at the wall,' he continued as he shone the small beam of light into Martin Kent's eye. 'Were you wearing protective goggles while you were making this bookcase?'

'I didn't think I needed to. I wear glasses all the time, you see, and I thought they'd be enough protection.'

Ben sighed. 'Sister, could you get me some fluorescein, please?'

'Have I....? Do you think I'm going to lose the sight in that eye, Doctor?' Martin Kent asked tremulously as Izzie went to get it.

'Let's not start crossing bridges until we come to them,' Ben said firmly.

'But it hurts so much,' Martin declared as Izzie returned. 'And it keeps watering all the time.'

'Actually, that can be a good sign,' Ben said encouragingly as he gently inserted some of the orange stain into Martin Kent's right eye. 'If you had no symptoms at all it could mean that whatever has gone into your eye has penetrated the cornea. Now, could you stare over my right shoulder again for me?'

Awkwardly Martin did as he asked.

'There's definitely a splinter in there,' Ben murmured. 'Luckily it seems to be lying on the surface of the cornea. Sister, I'll need—'

'Anaesthetic eye drops and a spatula,' she interrupted evenly. 'I've already brought them, Mr Farrell.'

He took them from her without a word but he was impressed. The head of Human Resources had said Izzie Clark was good, and she was—very good.

Deftly he inserted the eye drops and then shot her a quick, sidelong glance. He wondered what she saw in a man like Steve Melville. He was handsome certainly, but personally he found him a bit too glib, a bit too smooth, but he supposed it was all a matter of taste. His lips twisted slightly. He should know better than most that when it came to falling in love, sanity and common sense went straight out of the window.

'There's no need to look so worried, Mr Kent,' he declared with a smile as he picked up the tiny spatula. 'All you have to do is keep as still for me as you can.'

Martin Kent swallowed. 'Couldn't you zonk me out with something, Doc? It's not that I'm chicken or anything, but the thought of you digging around in my eye with that thing…'

'Would it help if I held your hand?' Izzie suggested.

Martin nodded fervently, and as he gripped Izzie's hand tightly Ben felt an unexpected twinge of envy.

She was a nice girl. Perhaps she was a bit too outspoken

for her own good, but she was still a nice girl. And she had the most amazing hair he'd ever seen. It was so thick and curly, and he found himself wondering how long it was—shoulder-length, longer? He'd love to see it down, and as for running his fingers through it…

Careful, Ben, he told himself as she unexpectedly glanced up and smiled at him. You were a fool once where a woman was concerned, and you should have learned your lesson by now.

'OK, Mr Kent,' he declared, 'I want you to stare at that mirror over my shoulder and keep very, very still. Good, good… You're doing marvellously… Keep staring at the mirror… Just a few seconds more… Got it!'

'Is it out?' Martin Kent said uncertainly, squinting up at Izzie.

'It is, indeed.' She nodded as she carefully slipped an eye patch over his head.

'But it still hurts,' he protested.

'I'm afraid it's going to hurt for quite a while,' Ben observed. 'Our receptionist will arrange an appointment for you at our ophthalmology clinic, but meanwhile keep that eye patch on and get your wife to insert these antibiotic eye drops four times a day.'

'Keep the patch on?' Martin Kent repeated in dismay as he got to his feet. 'But, Doctor, I'm a draughtsman—how can I work, using only one eye?'

'Be thankful it will eventually get better,' Ben declared. 'A millimetre deeper and you could have been blinded.'

Martin Kent blenched. 'It was that close?'

Ben nodded. 'Take my advice—wear protective goggles from now on when you're doing *any* kind of DIY.'

Gently Izzie helped Mr Kent along to Reception, but she'd scarcely returned to the treatment room when Steve steered her to one side.

'What's this with you and Mr Farrell getting all chummy

in the canteen?' He grinned. 'Is it Help the Aged Week or something?'

'That's not funny, Steve,' she protested.

'Izzie, the guy's forty—he's damn near old enough to be your father.'

'Only if he'd been a remarkably precocious fourteen-year-old,' she retorted, unaccountably irritated. 'Look, why won't you give the man a break? He's actually quite nice when you get to know him.'

A frown appeared in Steve's deep blue eyes. 'I didn't realise you had a secret thing for older men. Getting interested in him, are you?'

'Of course I'm not,' she hissed, uncomfortably aware that Ben Farrell was watching them from across the room. 'All I'm saying is it might be better if you gave him a chance instead of carping about him all the time.'

'I wasn't aware that I did,' he said stiffly, 'but if my presence is annoying you I'll make myself scarce.'

'I didn't say that,' she exclaimed with exasperation. 'But don't you think life would be a lot pleasanter if we all tried to get along?'

'Always the little peacemaker, aren't you, Izzie?' Steve replied drily.

She gazed at him uncertainly. She didn't want to fight with him—she loved him—but he wasn't being fair, and her innate sense of justice refused to be stilled.

'Maybe I am,' she said slowly, 'but surely that's better than stirring it all the time.'

His eyebrows snapped down. 'I thought you'd be on my side.'

'It's not a question of taking sides. It's just...' She shook her head. 'Oh, Steve, this isn't like you. You're usually so easygoing and reasonable. Can't you at least try to get on with him?'

For a moment he said nothing and then a small smile curved his lips. 'OK. We'll play it your way for a while, babe, but when Ben Farrell turns round and bites your head off don't say that I didn't warn you.'

It was all the fault of these damn exams, Izzie thought with a sigh as he walked away. He so desperately wanted to pass and she wouldn't be at all surprised if he wasn't eating properly, far less sleeping. Once they were over he'd go back to being the Steve she knew and loved...she knew he would.

'Babe?'

A faint flush of colour crept across her cheeks as she looked up to see Ben Farrell regarding her, his eyebrows raised. How much of their conversation had he heard? She hoped it wasn't much—she fervently prayed it wasn't much.

'Steve sometimes calls me that,' she said uncomfortably. 'It's only a term of endearment.'

'An odd one for a grown woman,' he observed. 'Babe's the last thing I'd call you if I were in love with you.'

Determinedly she resisted the impulse to ask what he would call her if he was in love with her.

'Problems, Tess?' he questioned as the student nurse joined them, looking distinctly flustered.

'There's a six-year-old in 1 with a suspected fractured wrist and I can't seem to find Dr Melville.'

A slight frown appeared on Ben's forehead and then he nodded. 'OK, Nurse Golding. Sister Clark, would you assist, please?'

Izzie followed him into the cubicle, all too conscious of Tess's disappointed gaze. A fractured wrist was hardly the most difficult of injuries to treat and Tess could quite easily have assisted him but it wasn't her place to say so.

Mrs Simpson, on the contrary, had plenty to say.

'I've told him time and time again not to climb the trees in the garden,' she exclaimed as Ben gently examined the boy's hand and wrist. 'But does he listen? No, he doesn't. Honestly, that boy—'

'Does your head hurt at all, Joey?' Ben interrupted, crouching down in front of the white-faced child who hadn't said a word throughout the examination. 'Any pain in your side or in your tummy when you take in a big breath?'

'I know what you're thinking, Doctor,' Mrs Simpson said quickly, 'but he didn't lose consciousness and, as you can see for yourself, he's breathing quite normally.'

'I think we'll give him a quick check-up to be on the safe side,' Ben observed. 'Sister Clark, would you take his clothes off for me?'

'Is that really necessary?' Mrs Simpson protested. 'His poor wrist's so sore—and we had to wait so long in Reception—'

'His clothes, Sister Clark,' Ben repeated firmly.

Izzie glanced curiously across at him. It hardly seemed necessary—even she could see that the wrist was fractured—but Ben just stared back at her impassively, and with a tiny shrug she gently eased off Joey's T-shirt, shorts and underwear.

'Would you take a deep breath for me, Joey?' Ben said as he placed his stethoscope on the child's thin chest. 'Well done. Once more…and again.'

'I told you it was only his wrist, didn't I, Doctor?' Mrs Simpson asserted as Ben gazed thoughtfully down at the child.

'Do you fall a lot, Joey?' he asked, running his finger lightly along an old bruise on the little boy's arm and another on his leg.

'You wouldn't believe how often.' Mrs Simpson laughed. 'Joey's got to be the most accident-prone child in the world. I keep telling my husband that if this goes on we'll have the social work people at our door.'

Izzie chuckled but Ben, she noticed, didn't. In fact, his grey eyes were totally expressionless as he asked, 'And what does your husband say to that, Mrs Simpson?'

'That boys will be boys,' she replied. 'And if this is the worst that happens to him we should think ourselves lucky.'

'Very true,' he said drily. 'OK, Sister, would you help Joey get dressed again?'

Swiftly Izzie did as he asked, though she would have been a whole lot faster if Joey's mother hadn't insisted on helping her.

'I'm pretty certain his wrist is fractured,' Ben declared when Joey was finally dressed. 'Sister Clark will arrange for a porter to take him along to X-Ray, and if it is fractured I'm afraid he's going to be in plaster for a few weeks.'

'That'll put an end to your tree-climbing expeditions, my lad,' Mrs Simpson declared, ruffling her son's blond hair affectionately.

It didn't take Izzie long to find a porter, and with Joey and his mother safely despatched to X-Ray she began erasing his name from the whiteboard—only to notice that Ben was standing in the centre of the treatment room, a pensive frown on his forehead.

'Something wrong?' she asked, putting down the eraser.

'According to our records this is the third time that little chap's been admitted this year. He had a fractured rib in January and a fractured ankle in April.'

'You don't think he could have osteogenesis imperfecta, do you?' she said with concern. 'Brittle-bone disease? We could organise a scan—'

'Did you see those bruises on his body?'

She gazed at him blankly for a moment and then dawning comprehension hit her.

'You think his parents are abusing him, don't you?' she gasped. 'Oh, Mr Farrell, that's ridiculous. Every child has accidents. I was forever tumbling out of trees, or off walls, when I was small.'

'So you were a tomboy, were you?' he said with an unexpected smile, but she refused to be sidetracked.

'Laura Simpson teaches in one of the local primary

schools. Her husband Scott's a solicitor. They're not the type—'

'So there's a type, is there?' he interrupted drily.

'No, of course there isn't,' she protested, 'but you saw how worried Laura was. She refused to leave his side for a minute.'

'Yes, I did notice that.'

'Oh, now you're suggesting she was trying to hide something,' she snapped with exasperation. 'She was concerned about Joey—mothers generally are concerned about their children, you know—and he's their only child.'

'Izzie, there's concern, and there's trying to make damn sure someone doesn't say anything.'

It was the first time he'd called her by her first name but she was far too angry to wonder at it.

'Mr Farrell, I've lived in this town all my life and, believe me, if there'd been a problem I'd have heard about it!'

He held up his hands in defeat. 'OK, OK, I'll bow to your superior local knowledge this time, but if that child comes back in again with so much as a cut finger I want to know about it.'

'I'll make sure that you do,' she retorted. 'I may seem like nothing more than a country hick to you but I'm not stupid!'

A slight smile curved his lips. 'I never said you were, but maybe—just maybe—you're a little bit too trusting for your own good.'

An angry retort sprang to her lips but before she could deliver it he had walked away and she glared angrily after him. He was wrong about Joey—she was positive he was. Scott and Lorna would never harm their son—everyone knew they adored him—and as for saying she was too trusting... She might have lived in Kelso all her life but that didn't make her naïve.

'Still think Mr Farrell's wonderful, do you?'

She whirled round to see Steve, grinning at her, and opened her mouth to reply but she didn't get a chance to. Fran was running down the room towards them.

'Priority on the way—man knocked down by a lorry in front of the supermarket in town. Chest injuries, head injury, abdominal injuries—you name it, this poor bloke's got it, and he'll be with us in five minutes.'

'OK, what casualties have we got waiting in Reception?' Ben said, appearing without warning beside them.

'Nobody that can't wait,' the staff nurse declared.

'Right. Alert Theatre and the surgical reg to be on standby. Tess, tell the lab I want six units O-negative and a CBC, and then be ready to get the patient's blood samples cross-matched.'

Tess turned to go and then stopped. 'How do we know the patient's O-negative, Mr Farrell?'

'We don't. O-negative's what we call the universal donor,' he explained as she gazed at him, puzzled. 'It can be given to any patient if we're in a life-threatening situation and it will buy us some time while we get a cross-match.'

'What do you want me to do?' Izzie asked as Tess dashed out of the treatment room.

'Check the emergency room and make sure—'

The rest of what he'd been about to say died in his throat as the doors to A and E swung open. The ambulance must have broken every speed limit in the book because the paramedics were already wheeling in their stretcher.

'We're losing him, Doc!' one of them shouted as they raced past them towards the emergency room. 'BP 60 over 40, no breath sounds, level of consciousness 7 on the Glasgow coma scale.'

'So what's the bad news?' Ben declared with a tight smile as he followed them. 'Fran, take the blood samples and get them along to the lab and tell them I want a count and blood match *now*. Izzie, connect the heart monitor and then get his clothes off. Steve—where the hell's Steve?'

'Here,' he replied with irritation.

'Connect the oxygen machine to Mr…Mr… Does anyone know this man's name?' Ben snapped as he swiftly inserted a fresh intravenous drip.

'It's Johnson—Tom Johnson,' one of the paramedics replied, pausing on his way out.

'Steve, get Mr Johnson connected to the oxygen machine and keep an eye on this drip. What's the BP now, Izzie?'

'Eighty over forty.'

'Pulse?'

'Fifty and dropping.'

'Tom—Tom, can you hear me?' Ben asked, bending his head to the man's lips.

A low moan was his only reply.

'I think his leg and pelvis are broken,' Steve observed.

'Frankly I'd say that's the least of his worries right now,' Ben replied, his voice tight. 'Is there any sign of the surgical reg?'

'Not yet,' Fran said breathlessly as she joined them. I've had him paged, but—'

'He's arresting!' Izzie exclaimed.

Swiftly Ben injected some lignocaine into a vein in Tom Johnson's arm, and then lifted the paddles connected to the defibrillator. 'Stand back, everyone.'

Quickly they all stepped back from the trolley, and as Ben applied the metal plates to Tom Johnson's chest every eye was fixed to the heart monitor.

'No change,' Izzie declared as Tom Johnson's inert body convulsed briefly from the effect of the electrical shock.

'Come on, Tom…come on,' Ben murmured as he reapplied the plates. 'Breathe, damn you, breathe.'

Izzie stared at the monitor, willing it to spring into life, to start recording a heartbeat, however erratic, but it stayed resolutely level.

'Still nothing,' she muttered.

'Maybe third time lucky,' Ben said grimly, laying the paddles against the sides of Tom Johnson's chest again.

'We've got him!' Izzie exclaimed with a surge of relief as the heart monitor sprang into life. 'Heartbeat faint and erratic, but it's there.'

'OK, now we're rolling,' Ben declared. 'BP, Izzie?'

'Seventy over forty.'

'Start an IV dopamine drip. Steve—clean up his face and head, and yell out if you find anything that worries you. Staff—Staff, where's that damn blood?'

'It's here!' she said as one of the lab technicians appeared at the door.

'Right, start pumping it into him. Izzie, watch his vital signs while I try to stem the bleeding in his chest. One of his ribs has punctured a lung, and the last thing we want is it collapsing on us.'

He was good, Izzie thought as she watched him. Nothing flapped him, nothing threw him, and for such a big man he was remarkably quick on his feet.

As though suddenly aware of her gaze, he looked up and smiled. 'This is one hell of a way to make a living, isn't it?'

She blinked and then chuckled. So he did have a sense of humour, but how he could joke at a time like this was beyond her. He must have nerves of steel.

'OK, everyone,' he said at last. 'That's the best we can do. This guy needs the theatre and fast. Has the surgical reg arrived yet, or is he still out on the golf course?'

Izzie shot him a warning glance. Mr Evanton had just appeared in the doorway and he was notorious throughout the hospital for his total lack of humour, but Ben seemed totally unperturbed.

'Glad you could spare the time to join us, Evanton,' he exclaimed, turning towards him. 'Got our message eventually, did you?'

'I'll take over now, Mr Farrell,' he replied tightly.

'Be my guest,' Ben said, pulling off his surgical gloves. 'OK, folks,' he added as Fran and Steve gazed at him uncertainly. 'Show's over, and we've still got patients waiting out there.'

Izzie waited until they were alone, before shaking her head at him. 'Rubbing Mr Evanton up the wrong way isn't exactly the best way to win friends and influence at the Kelso General, you know.'

'It needed saying, Izzie,' he declared. 'It took him fifteen minutes to get here—fifteen minutes!'

'I agree it's far too long,' she said, 'but, please, don't make a habit of antagonising the other consultants at the hospital. They're a close-knit bunch, and they could make life very uncomfortable for you.'

He shrugged. 'I can live with it.'

She shook her head again as she watched him swing out of the emergency room. He was such a strange man—a man full of contradictions—and yet she liked him. She didn't quite know why, but she did.

She glanced up at the clock. Their shift had ended an hour ago, and quickly she made her way to the staffroom.

'Boy, am I bushed,' Steve exclaimed when he saw her. 'Why don't we all go out for a drink—relax together?'

'Sorry,' Fran replied as she threw on her cardigan and made for the door. 'My husband will have my dinner ready and he'll go apoplectic if I'm late home again.'

'What about you, Tess?' Steve asked.

The student nurse ran her hand through her short, spiky, black hair apologetically. 'No can do, I'm afraid. I've got a date.'

Izzie gazed pointedly at Steve. Ben had appeared at the staffroom door and with an elaborate sigh Steve turned to him obediently.

'What about you, Mr Farrell?' he asked. 'Would you like to come for a drink with Izzie and me?'

For a second Izzie thought he was going to agree but

then he shook his head. 'Two's company, three's a crowd, and I'm not really a pub person anyway. Thanks for asking, though,' he added as he picked up a file from the coffee-table and disappeared back through the door.

Izzie gazed after him wistfully. If ever a man looked in serious need of company it was Ben Farrell and yet, according to Fran, he lived alone in Keeper's Cottage on the outskirts of town.

She pulled herself up short as she found herself picturing him returning home to an empty house. What the hell was she doing? She was going home to an empty flat and yet she didn't feel miserable and lonely when she opened the door. Well, actually, yes, she did, she thought, and unconsciously shook her head. Get a grip, Izzie Clark, or the next thing you'll be doing is turning up on the man's doorstep with a casserole.

'Izzie, that guy's seriously weird,' Steve observed as he followed the direction of her gaze.

'Lots of people don't like pubs,' she declared, reaching for her handbag.

'Every guy likes pubs,' he said firmly.

She leaned her head against the wall and pretended to snore but to no avail.

'I mean it, Izzie,' he continued. 'There's something really odd about that guy. What's he doing here, for a start?'

'The same as we are—working.'

'But Farrell was a consultant at the Newcastle Infirmary.'

'And you came to Kelso from Edinburgh,' she pointed out.

'Yes, but I came because it was a promotion for me. It's not a promotion for Farrell—ye gods, it's practically a *de*motion.'

Izzie shook her head as she took her jacket down from behind the door. 'Maybe he likes the country—maybe he just simply wanted a change.'

'Yeah, right,' Steve said cynically, and Izzie rolled her eyes heavenwards.

'You know, I'm getting seriously worried about you,' she observed. 'The next thing you'll be telling me is that Ben Farrell's secretly a modern-day Dr Crippen with a string of dead girlfriends left behind in Newcastle.'

'OK, OK,' he replied as he followed her out into the corridor, 'you can mock all you like, but that guy came here for a reason, and I'll bet my stethoscope it wasn't for the change of air!'

CHAPTER THREE

'YOU'D think people would realise by now just how damn dangerous too much sun can be,' Ben declared with irritation as he pulled off his surgical gloves. 'That's the fourth case of sunburn we've seen in two days.'

'I know,' Izzie replied as she stripped the paper sheet from the trolley in cubicle 6, 'but you can't really blame people for wanting to go out and make the most of this hot spell.'

'I can if it means they're going to end up with skin cancer in a few years' time,' he fumed, and then frowned as the sound of raised voices drifted across to them from one of the cubicles. 'What the hell's going on out there?'

Izzie tilted her head and listened. One of the voices—a female's—sounded oddly familiar, while the other clearly belonged to a very angry Steve. 'It's probably a drunk.'

'At this time in the afternoon?' Ben protested.

'Some people would drink all day if they could.' Izzie sighed as she went out into the treatment room and quickly motioned to Fran. 'What's the problem?'

'Female casualty who swears she's hurt her foot. Steve can't find anything wrong with it, and now she's demanding to see someone in authority.'

Izzie's eyebrows rose. 'Is she one of our regular troublemakers?'

'I don't recognise her,' Fran answered, 'but she says she knows you.'

Izzie's eyebrows rose even higher and swiftly she strode into the cubicle to find herself staring down into Joanna Ogilvy's lovely but irate face.

'Izzie!' she exclaimed, pushing Steve aside to envelop

41

her in a perfumed hug. 'Thank God for a friendly face. I've been trying to explain to this nurse here that I'm in absolute agony but the silly man just doesn't seem to understand!'

Over the top of her head, Steve drew his finger expressively across his throat and Izzie choked.

'Mr Melville isn't a nurse, Joanna,' she said with as much composure as she could. 'He's our senior house officer.'

'Oh, I'm terribly sorry,' she declared contritely, flashing Steve an enchanting smile, 'but I really think—no offence intended to you—I should see someone more senior. I can hardly put any weight on this foot.'

'We could ask the orthopaedic consultant to come down and take a look at it,' Izzie said dubiously, 'but Mr Farrell would have to OK that first.'

Joanna's face lit up. 'Oh, please, send for Mr Farrell—I'm sure he'll know exactly what to do.'

Quickly Izzie stepped back through the curtains and Steve followed her.

'Izzie, there's not a damn thing wrong with her foot,' he muttered in an undertone.

'I know.' She laughed.

'Then why ask Farrell to take a look at her?'

'Female intuition,' she replied, her eyes dancing. 'Don't ask me to explain it,' she added as he opened his mouth, clearly intending to do just that. 'Let's just say I have a feeling this is one for the boss.'

'What's one for the boss?' a deep male voice asked behind her.

'The patient in 1, Mr Farrell,' she answered, turning to face him, her features carefully re-arranged into an expression of schoolgirl innocence. 'There seems to be some problem with her foot and Dr Melville would like a second opinion.'

'Then he's got a very odd way of showing it,' Ben observed as Steve beat a hasty retreat. 'What's going on, Izzie?'

'Nothing,' she said, trying and failing to stop the corners of her mouth from lifting. 'It's just that Dr Melville and I feel this particular casualty requires your very special expertise.'

He studied her face for a moment and then his lips quirked. 'You've got the Secretary of State for Health in there, right?'

A gurgle of laughter broke from her. 'Somebody a whole lot more important, believe me. It's—'

She didn't get the chance to say any more. The curtains around the cubicle were suddenly thrown open and Joanna appeared, her face wreathed in smiles.

'Mr Farrell!' she exclaimed. 'Thank you so much for coming.'

'What seems to be the trouble, Miss...Miss...?'

'It's Joanna.' She beamed. 'We've met before, remember?'

'Have we?' Ben said absently as he guided her back into the cubicle.

A flash of annoyance appeared in Joanna's large green eyes and Izzie had to struggle hard to stifle the laughter that threatened to overwhelm her. That her old schoolfriend wasn't used to being forgotten was plain, and that she didn't like it was obvious.

'Surely you must remember,' Joanna declared plaintively. 'I brought my father in last week when he'd hurt his thumb.'

'I'm afraid we see rather a lot of patients, Miss...Miss... What did you say your name was again?' Ben asked as he crouched down in front of Joanna.

'Ogilvy,' she exclaimed through perfect white teeth. 'Joanna Ogilvy. Izzie and I went to school together.'

'Did you?' Ben said without apparent interest as he

gently began prodding the base of her foot. 'Does this hurt?'

She nodded. 'A little. But where it really hurts,' she added, lifting the hem of her long floral skirt to reveal a suntanned slender calf, 'is round about here.'

God, she was so obvious, Izzie thought with a flash of irritation, but, then, she always had been. Joanna the Man-Eater was what they'd nicknamed her at school, and she clearly hadn't changed one bit. And they'd never been friends, she remembered now. Joanna didn't have female friends, only potential rivals.

She sighed inwardly as she gazed down at Ben's lowered head. The poor man wouldn't stand a chance against a practised seductress like Joanna, but just as she came to that conclusion he suddenly glanced up and winked at her. Maybe he wouldn't be such a push-over after all, she thought with a smile of delight. Maybe Joanna had finally met her match at last.

'What kind of shoes do you normally wear, Miss Ogilvy?' Ben asked as he stood up.

'High heels, of course. They're so very flattering to the leg, don't you think?' she added with a megawatt smile.

'It's not something I've given much consideration to,' he observed. 'It looks to me as though you've strained your gastrocnemius muscle. Wear flat shoes for a couple of weeks and that should cure it.'

'But flat shoes are so ugly,' she pouted, gazing pointedly at Izzie's regulation lace-ups. 'And I've got tickets for a charity ball next weekend at Manderston. I can't possibly wear flat shoes to that.'

'I can only give you my advice,' Ben declared as he turned to go. 'Whether you take it or not is up to you.'

Quickly Joanna caught hold of his hand. 'The charity ball—I've got two tickets for it.'

'And you'd like Sister Clark to go with you?' he said with apparent delight. 'How very kind.'

Joanna all but ground her teeth. 'Mr Farrell—'

'Sorry to interrupt,' Fran said as her head came round the cubicle curtains, 'but we've got an RTA on the way.'

'Any details?' Ben asked, and strode out of the cubicle quickly, leaving Joanna gazing impotently after him.

'Man and woman,' Fran replied. 'Their car skidded off the Kelso to Jedburgh road and the woman seems to be the most badly injured. Extensive facial injuries and some trouble with her breathing.'

'Alert Ed Harvey in plastic surgery, and the surgical reg, and tell the lab I'll probably be needing four units of cross-matched,' Ben declared. 'When's the ETA?'

'Fifteen minutes.'

'He consulted the whiteboard. 'That should just about give us time to clear the decks.'

It was scarcely enough. Izzie had barely finished dressing the badly scalded hand of one of the local children when the wailing siren of the ambulance alerted her to its arrival.

'That's you, Melanie,' she smiled, helping the child down from the trolley. 'If your hand starts to swell, or if it feels tender, go to your doctor right away. Oh, and Melanie,' she added, 'in future leave any cooking to your mum or dad—OK?'

The little girl nodded, and her mother rolled her eyes heavenwards in an attitude of 'Who'd ever be a parent?' Izzie chuckled as she headed out into the treatment room.

Her laughter died, however, when the paramedics wheeled in their two stretchers. They'd been right when they'd said the woman had received the worst of the injuries. Her face was barely recognisable as a face any more, and from her laboured breathing Izzie guessed that one of her lungs was partially collapsed.

'The woman's Maria Mackinlay, the man's George Haig,' one of the paramedics informed them as they eased the young woman off the stretcher and onto a trolley.

'Friends, relations, colleagues?' Ben asked, deftly inserting a fresh haemeccel drip as Izzie quickly began cutting off as much of Maria Mackinlay's clothing as she could.

'Mr Haig's most reluctant to give us his home telephone number so we're guessing he and Miss Mackinlay are rather more than friends and his wife doesn't know about it.'

'I see,' Ben said tightly. 'Any idea what happened?'

'He swerved to avoid another car and she went straight through the windscreen.'

Ben shook his head. 'Why, oh, why won't people wear seat belts?'

'She was wearing one,' the paramedic observed, 'but she took it off to try to persuade Mr Haig to slow down. He's drunk, you see.'

A muttered oath came from Ben as he placed his stethoscope on Maria's chest. 'I'm not getting any breath sounds on the right side.'

'We intubated her when we arrived at the scene,' the paramedic continued, 'but—'

'Her trachea is shifting to the left,' Ben finished for him. 'OK, Steve—you take the man. It looks like mostly superficial cuts to me but yell out if you need help.'

'Her BP's 60 over 40, Mr Farrell,' Izzie warned.

Air was clearly seeping into Maria's chest every time she took a breath but it wasn't coming out again. A large bubble of air was being created and it was pressing on the collapsed lung. If they didn't correct it—and fast—her heart and blood vessels would be compressed and no blood would reach her brain.

Deftly Ben stabbed a needle into Maria's upper chest to release the air bubble, but they still needed to re-inflate the lung and evacuate any blood from the chest. With one swift movement Ben made a small incision into Maria's chest and inserted a chest-tube.

'BP stabilising, trachea shifting back,' Izzie declared with relief.

'OK, I'll continue aspirating her while you pick out as much of the glass from her face as you can,' Ben exclaimed. 'But go carefully.'

Izzie nodded, but it was a slow and heart-breaking task. Maria's broken nose would mend, and her fractured jaw and smashed cheek-bone could be realigned, but not even the most expert plastic surgery would give her back the face she'd once had.

'She must have been a very pretty girl,' she murmured when Ben leant over to check on her efforts.

'"Must have been" being the key words,' he said, his voice oddly flat as the bulky form of Kelso General's Head of Plastic Surgery appeared through the cubicle curtains.

'What's the situation?' Ed Harvey asked.

'Tension pneumothorax,' Ben replied, 'but I've aspirated her, and the lung seems stable now. The worst damage is to her face.'

'So I see.' Ed sighed, but as he made to follow the porter who'd begun wheeling Maria Mackinlay out of the treatment room Ben caught hold of his arm.

'Miss Mackinlay—you'll do your best for her, won't you?'

'Hey, has no one told you that my stitching would make the creators of the Bayeux Tapestry green with envy?' Ed protested.

A small smile appeared on Ben's lips but it disappeared as soon as Ed Harvey had gone.

'You should take a break,' Izzie observed, seeing the fatigue in his face as she stripped off her bloodstained surgical gloves. 'Steve can handle—'

'Is the driver still here?'

Something about his tone made her unaccountably uneasy. 'I should imagine so. The police will be wanting to interview—'

She was talking to thin air. Ben was already striding away and, without knowing why, she instinctively followed him.

'I'm almost finished,' Steve declared as Ben swept into the cubicle. 'Apart from a broken collar-bone, it's just minor cuts and bruises.'

'I'm sure Miss Mackinlay will be overjoyed to hear that,' Ben said, his voice ice-cold.

'How is she?' George Haig asked, wincing as he eased himself up into a sitting position. 'Is she OK?'

'We've just sent her up to Theatre,' Ben replied. 'With luck, our plastic surgeon should be able to put her face back together again—though whether you'll recognise her is another matter.'

Mr Haig whitened. 'But she is going to be OK, isn't she? I mean, she's not going to die?'

'No, she's not going to die,' Ben exclaimed, 'but she's going to need a lot of counselling to help her get over her changed appearance.'

A deep flush of colour appeared on Mr Haig's face. 'It was an accident—'

'Save your explanation for the police,' Ben interrupted. 'What I want is your home telephone number and the name of someone we can contact on Miss Mackinlay's behalf.'

'Is that strictly necessary?' George Haig said awkwardly. 'I'm OK, and you said Maria was going to be all right—'

'She is, but she's probably going to be in hospital for quite some considerable time. Don't you think she might like to have someone who truly cares about her visiting occasionally?'

Ben's tone was biting and George Haig coloured even more.

'Her parents live in Essex,' he said uncomfortably, 'but they're quite elderly. Surely we don't have to upset them unnecessarily? If it's a question of money…'

Ben's eyebrows snapped down. 'Money?'

'Hospital fees, that sort of thing. I'm quite prepared to pay—'

'This is the NHS, Mr Haig,' Ben broke in coldly. 'There's no question of payment so if we could have those two telephone numbers, please?'

George Haig stared down at his hands. 'Look, the thing is, my wife doesn't know about Maria, and if you phone Maria's parents, and they come up, they're bound to ask a lot of awkward questions—'

'*Awkward* questions?' Ben spat out. 'Maybe you should have thought of *awkward* questions before you cheated on your wife! Maybe you should have thought of *awkward* questions before you got into your car blind drunk!'

Out of the corner of her eye Izzie could see Steve staring at Ben in appalled horror and she took a step forward quickly. 'Mr Farrell—'

'Men like you don't ever think of the consequences of their actions, do they?' he continued as though she hadn't spoken, his grey eyes dark with fury. 'They just live for today and to hell with the consequences. You could have killed that young woman today and, believe me, when she recovers and looks at her face—'

'Mr Farrell, *please*!'

In desperation Izzie had caught hold of his sleeve and he whirled round on her, his face furious. 'What? What do you want?'

Never had she seen such anger on anyone's face before and she had to take a deep breath before she could speak.

'I think…' she began hesitantly. 'I think Staff Nurse Walton is calling for you.'

He almost sent her flying as he brushed past her out of the cubicle and she had to take another breath to steady herself. Please, God, she prayed, let him come to his senses and calm down when he discovers that Fran doesn't want him—or I don't know what I'm going to do.

'What the heck was that all about?' Steve muttered as George Haig lay back on his pillow, shocked and silent.

Determinedly Izzie began binning the soiled swabs that he had used. 'It's none of our business.'

'But Farrell—the way he behaved. Talk about unethical—'

'And you've never lost your temper?' she snapped. 'Never had a bad day?'

'Hey, don't bite my head off,' Steve protested. 'I'm not the one who went ballistic.'

She marched through the curtains into the treatment room, only to groan as she heard the sound of raised voices coming from Reception. God in heaven, what now? she thought as she ran through the swing doors, just in time to see Mavis disappearing out of A and E like a frightened rabbit while Ben loomed over their receptionist with a face like thunder.

'What is it? What's wrong?' Izzie asked, glancing from April to Ben, then back again.

'Mavis,' April began tearfully. 'He's found out that there's never anything wrong with Mavis.'

'Too right I have,' Ben stormed, apparently oblivious to the fascinated faces of the waiting casualties. 'What the hell do you mean by allowing her to hang around here all the time? A and E's not some form of cheap entertainment when there's nothing interesting on TV!'

Izzie gazed at him silently. Sweet reason would get her nowhere. There was only one thing she could do, and she did it. She caught hold of his arm and began dragging him back through the swing doors.

'What the hell do you think you're doing?' he demanded, throwing off her hand.

'What it looks like,' she answered crisply. 'Trying to get you back to your office before you completely forget yourself and hit somebody.'

For one awful moment she thought that she might be

that somebody. His face was so furious that all her instincts told her to run, but she stood her ground, meeting him glare for glare, until he suddenly turned on his heel and slammed through the doors, leaving her gazing white-faced and trembling after him.

'Izzie?'

She managed a wobbly smile at the receptionist. 'No, I haven't got the faintest idea of what that was all about, April, but I'm definitely going to find out.'

It was one thing to voice such determination, however, and quite another to put it into practice. By the time she'd reached his office her resolution had all but deserted her. Maybe this wasn't such a good idea. Maybe she should just go away and forget all about it. But he's upset, her heart said, he might welcome company. And then again he might just give you an earful for your pains, her mind replied.

Well, there was only one way to find out and, squaring her shoulders, she took a deep breath and opened the door.

He didn't even move at her entrance. He just stayed where he was, gazing out of the window, and she took a hesitant step forward. 'Mr Farrell, are you OK?'

'What kind of a damn fool question is that?' he snapped.

'A perfectly reasonable one, I'd have thought,' she answered evenly, though a faint tinge of colour appeared on her cheeks. 'You yell at a patient—'

'He was drunk.'

'Yes, he was drunk, but we're not here to make moral judgements. Then you yell at a little old lady whose only fault is being lonely—'

She came to a halt. He'd turned to face her as she'd been speaking, and there was such raw pain on his face that instinctively she moved towards him then stopped as he held up his hand.

'You're right,' he said raggedly. 'I know I shouldn't have lost my temper, but you see…' His face twisted. 'My wife… My wife was killed by a drunk driver.'

'Oh, Ben, I'm so sorry,' she said softly, using his first name without thinking, but he didn't seem to notice.

Instead, he closed his eyes and leaned his head against the window. For a second she gazed indecisively at him. If he'd been a patient or a relative she'd immediately have gone to him and put her arms around him. Well, so what if he wasn't a patient or a relative? He clearly needed comfort.

'I'm so very sorry,' she murmured, wrapping her arms around him. 'I know that's a pretty inadequate thing to say—'

She scarcely had time to register that his shoulders were as broad as they looked, that his chest was as deep, before he wrenched himself free from her grasp.

'Not inadequate,' he said stiffly, his hand going to the knot in his tie as though his collar was suddenly too tight. 'Just unnecessary. It happened two years ago. It's best forgotten.'

But you haven't forgotten it, she thought, studying his drawn face. You remember it as though it were yesterday.

'If you ever want to talk, I'm a very good listener,' she said gently.

He shook his head. 'Talking changes nothing.'

'But—'

'I don't want your sympathy, Izzie,' he broke in harshly. 'I don't need it.'

'Everyone needs help some time,' she pointed out.

'Well, I don't,' he retorted. 'If you really want to make yourself useful, get back to work!'

His face was cold, his voice biting, and to her dismay she felt hot tears pricking at the back of her eyes. 'I'm sorry,' she muttered. 'Sorry that you feel I've butted in where I'm not wanted. I…I honestly didn't mean to.'

Blindly she made for the door, only to feel her arm suddenly caught and held.

'Oh, Izzie, I'm sorry,' he said, his voice husky. 'I know

you're only trying to help but you see…' He bunched his fists tightly against his sides, and when he spoke again it was with difficulty. 'I can't…I just can't bear sympathy.'

She stretched out a hand to him, then let it fall. There had to be something she could say that would give him comfort, but what?

'I think…' she said at last. 'I think we could both do with a cup of tea.'

'*Tea?*' He spat the word out bitterly then rubbed his hands roughly across his face as he saw the hurt in her eyes. 'I'm sorry, sorry. Tea…tea would be great.'

She reached for the doorhandle then paused.

'Will you…? Are you going to be all right while I go and get it?' she asked uncertainly.

A crooked smile appeared on his lips. 'I'm not going to slit my throat if that's what you mean.'

'Of course I didn't,' she replied stoutly. But I very much wondered if you might do someone grievous bodily harm, she added mentally as she made her way swiftly to the staffroom.

Just how wrong was it possible to be about somebody? she wondered as she switched on the kettle and put a couple of teabags in the teapot. Steve had said Ben Farrell was arrogant. She herself had initially thought him cold, but there was a world of pain inside him, pain that she prayed to God she'd never personally experience.

She reached for the biscuit tin and froze. Was that why he'd come to Kelso—he'd wanted to escape from his memories? It wouldn't have been what she'd have chosen to do. She'd have stayed amongst her friends and family, but perhaps he hadn't been able to do that and she couldn't help but wonder why.

'OK, what gives?'

She jumped and turned quickly to find herself gazing into Steve's deep blue eyes.

'That outburst over Mr Haig, I mean,' he continued when she said nothing. 'Did you find out what it was all about?'

She filled the teapot and put two cups on the tray. 'Yes, I did.'

'And?'

'And nothing. Mr Farrell spoke to me in confidence.'

'Of course he did,' he said in his best wheedling tone, 'but this is Steve talking, sweetie. We don't have secrets, remember?'

He was right. Normally they didn't, but this was different. 'I'm sorry, Steve, but I can't tell you.'

'Izzie—'

'It wouldn't be right, Steve,' she protested. 'Surely you can see that?'

For a moment he gazed at her, irritation plain on his face, and then a regretful smile appeared on his lips. 'I guess you're right. But, Izzie,' he continued as she made her way to the door, 'don't have too many secrets from me, OK? You're my girl, and a bloke can get jealous, you know.'

'Jealous?' she repeated. 'Of me and…?' She shook her head and laughed. 'That's the most ridiculous thing I've ever heard.'

And it was, she thought as she walked quickly back to Ben's office. Good grief, Steve might just as well be jealous of Ed Harvey and, nice man though Ed was, the portly plastic surgeon was hardly any girl's idea of Prince Charming.

'That was fast,' Ben said as she carried in the tray and put it down on his desk.

'Somebody had already boiled the kettle.' She shot him a quick glance. 'Are you…? I mean, do you feel any better now?'

'If you mean, have I calmed down, then, yes, I've calmed down.' A faint smile curved his lips. 'Look, you don't have to worry. I don't lose my temper every time I see a drunk driver.'

She flushed. In truth, that was exactly what she had been fearing. 'Then why—?'

'Did I react that way today?' He dragged his hands through his black hair and sighed as she began pouring out the tea. 'I honestly don't know. Maybe it was seeing that girl's face, knowing that it could so easily have been avoided—just as Caroline's death could have been avoided.'

'How long were you married?' she asked, sitting down opposite him.

'Five years.'

Scarcely any time at all for a love that had clearly been as deep as his.

'Mr Farrell—'

'You called me Ben before.'

· So he had noticed, she thought with dismay. 'I didn't mean to,' she floundered. 'It just sort of slipped—'

'I think you've earned the right to use it after what I've put you through today, don't you?' he broke in.

He was smiling and she found herself smiling back. He had a nice smile. Actually, he had a very nice smile indeed. And a nice mouth too—wide and soft and—

Quickly she took a gulp of tea. Boy, she must really be missing Steve if she was starting to find Ben Farrell physically attractive.

'As…as a friend,' she forced herself to say, 'could I make a suggestion?'

'What kind of suggestion?' he asked curiously.

'I think you should start mixing with people again.'

His eyebrows snapped down. 'Dating, you mean?'

'No, not dating as such,' she said hurriedly. 'Simply going out for a meal with someone or to the cinema.'

'With someone like your friend Joanna, you mean?' he observed, staring at her over the rim of his cup.

Absolutely not, her mind shrieked. Joanna is the very last person in the world I'd recommend you go out with.

'She isn't really my friend,' she murmured, 'but she does seem to like you.'

'She does, doesn't she?' he said, leaning back against his seat, his grey eyes fixed on her.

'And she is quite pretty,' Izzie said grudgingly. 'If...if you like redheads, that is.'

'My wife was a redhead.'

'Was she?' she said without enthusiasm. 'I suppose...I suppose she was small and beautiful, too, like Joanna?'

'Yes, yes, she was.'

She stared down at her tea. Why had she started this conversation? She'd only begun it to try to cheer him up and now she was the one who was feeling oddly depressed.

'I gather Joanna's divorced?' he observed.

Divorced and wearing a sign over her head that said 'Available to Anyone', Izzie thought waspishly.

'Yes, she's divorced,' she muttered.

He said nothing and she glanced up at him. Was that a smile, tugging at his lips? For a second it seemed it was and then it was gone.

'I'd better go,' she observed. 'The others must be wondering where I've got to.'

He stood up too and held out his hand. 'Thanks for getting me out of that mess earlier, Izzie. I owe you one.'

And I'll collect, believe me. The words sprang to her lips but she didn't say them. In fact, when his fingers enveloped hers, all thoughts of saying anything at all disappeared from her mind.

This is crazy, she thought, gazing up at him, all too aware that her heart was suddenly racing in a curiously disjointed fashion. I'm not interested in this man. I could never be interested in this man. OK, so he's got a nice smile and a nice mouth, and those flecks of grey in his hair are really attractive, but he's not my type and never could be. Then why are you blushing? a little voice whispered at the back of her mind, and you are, you know you are.

'I—I really must go,' she stammered, trying without success to extricate her hand. 'Steve and Fran—'

His fingers tightened around hers. 'Izzie, about Steve...'

'Steve?' she repeated, bewildered.

'You've been kind enough to give me some advice so could I give you some? Don't let him walk all over you the way he does.'

She blinked. 'Walk all over me?'

'The way he speaks to you, the way he patronises you—all this "babe" and "sweetie" rubbish. It's demeaning.'

She stared at him speechlessly, then dragged her hand free.

'Some people,' she exclaimed angrily. '*Some people* might find what he calls me rather sweet.'

'Would they?' he observed cryptically.

'Yes, yes, they would,' she retorted. 'And to say that he walks all over me... You know nothing about Steve and me—*nothing*—and even if you did, how I live my life is none of your damn business!'

A flash of anger appeared in his grey eyes and for a second she thought he was actually going to have the nerve to argue with her, then he nodded with difficulty. 'You're absolutely right.'

Too right she was, she fumed as she slammed out of his office. Steve didn't patronise her. He loved her, and she loved him. And as for saying he walked all over her... OK, so maybe there were times when she occasionally wondered if perhaps he didn't take her a little bit for granted but—

She pulled herself up short. What in the world was she thinking? Of course he didn't take her for granted. They were in love. They were going to get married one day.

'Izzie!'

She wheeled round, still angry, to see Steve coming out of the treatment room, and forced a smile to her lips. 'What can I do for you?'

'Make me happy,' he begged, encircling her waist with his arm and drawing her close. 'Let me come over to your place tonight.'

Her heart lifted, only to fall down again immediately. 'Oh, Steve, I'm sorry but you can't. I've invited Joan Stewart from Pathology over for dinner.'

'Then tell her to come tomorrow,' he coaxed, nibbling her ear gently. 'All work and no play is making Steve a very dull boy.'

'Steve, I can't.' She sighed regretfully. 'Joan's mother is really ill and she needs somebody to talk to.'

'And what about me?' he demanded, releasing her abruptly. 'I need somebody to talk to—or don't I count for anything any more?'

'Of course you do,' she protested, seeing the anger in his face. 'Look, come tomorrow night—'

'I've got a seminar tomorrow night.'

'Then Friday— Oh, sorry, not Friday—Fran and I are going to the cinema.'

'Becoming quite the little gadabout, aren't you, Izzie?' he said tersely. 'Oh, forget it,' he added as she opened her mouth to protest. 'Maybe you can pencil me in for a fortnight on Tuesday if you're not too busy!'

She bit her lip as he walked away. Never had she felt quite so much out of charity with him, and it was all Ben Farrell's fault. She wasn't altogether clear why it was Ben Farrell's fault but somehow it was, and as she swung through the doors of the treatment room she let out a low and highly colourful oath.

Men—who needed them?

CHAPTER FOUR

IZZIE sighed wistfully as she peered into the shop window. It was a stunning dress. Pale green silk, with a beaded fitted bodice, tiny shoulder straps and a skirt that billowed out like a dream. It would be just perfect for the dance after the hospital fair next week. It was also unfortunately rather a stunning price and with a deeper sigh she bent down and retrieved her groceries. It looked like she'd be wearing her old faithful blue dress again.

'Izzie—Izzie Clark!'

She glanced over her shoulder with a questioning lift of her eyebrows and groaned when she saw Ben Farrell crossing the street. Of all people to meet on her morning off, it would have to be him.

'You look laden,' he observed, gazing down at the carrier bags in her hands. 'Been shopping?'

No, I've been sky-diving, she thought sourly. Of course I've been shopping—any idiot could see that.

'I'm afraid you'll have to excuse me,' she replied, beginning to edge away, annoyingly aware that she must look a mess in the faded sundress she'd thrown on this morning, and even more annoyingly aware that she actually cared. 'But I'm in a bit of a hurry—'

'Must you rush off?' he said quickly. 'I'm just going for lunch and I was hoping you might join me. Please,' he continued, clearly sensing her reluctance. 'I know I'm in your black books after my remarks about Steve last week and I'd like to make it up to you.'

Tell him no, her mind urged. Tell him you're too busy, but his gaze was so earnest that before she could stop herself she heard herself saying, 'It would have to be a very quick lunch. I've got to be at the hospital by two.'

'So have I.' He smiled, taking the carrier bags from her hands. 'Where's your car? I'll stow these in the boot for you.'

'It's round the corner in Bridge Street unless the police have towed it away, thinking it's an abandoned wreck.'

His lips twitched. 'It's old?'

'Let's put it this way.' she sighed. 'Rumour has it Ben Hur had his first driving lesson in it.'

He threw back his head and laughed, but as they walked across the square together a slight frown appeared on his face as he shifted her bags in his hands. 'What in the world have you got in here—rocks?'

'It's my week's shopping. Look, let me carry one,' she added, only to see him shake his head. 'I usually buy as much as I can in one go—it saves having to shop after work.'

'Couldn't Steve have helped you with it?' he asked with more than a touch of irritation.

'He normally would have but he's moved back into the staff accommodation.'

He came to a halt, his eyes fixed on her. 'You've split up?'

'Of course not.' She laughed. 'He's studying for his exams and I think he found me a bit distracting.'

A slight smile curved his lips. 'I'm not surprised.'

'Hey, I'm not that noisy!' she protested.

'That's not what I meant.'

She looked up at him quickly, wondering what he *had* meant, but he suddenly seemed to be finding the buildings around the square particularly interesting.

'You know, every time I come into Kelso I'm reminded of Provence,' he observed.

'Provence?' she repeated, momentarily confused by the unexpected change in the conversation.

He nodded. 'If you added wooden shutters to the windows of the houses around the square we could be in a French town.'

'I've never been to France,' she replied as they turned left into Bridge Street. 'In fact, I've never been abroad at all.'

'What—never ever?' he said as she stopped beside the oldest Renault he had ever seen.

'With what the NHS pay me, I'm lucky not to be living in a cardboard box instead of in a rented flat over the bank, far less going on foreign holidays,' she said ruefully. 'And before you ask,' she added as he opened his mouth, 'yes, there have been times when I've been tempted to drill down through the floorboards.'

A dull flush of colour appeared on his cheeks.

'I'm sorry—I didn't think,' he muttered as he put her groceries into the boot of the car.

Her brown eyes twinkled. 'Rich doctors never do. Now, where are we going for lunch?'

He clasped her by the elbow and guided her back across the street. 'I thought the Ednam House.'

It was her turn to come to a halt. 'The Ednam House?'

'I stayed there for a week before I moved into my cottage and I can vouch for the food.'

'I'm sure you can,' she declared, 'but I'm hardly dressed for one of Kelso's poshest hotels, am I?'

'What's wrong with the way you're dressed?'

Typical male, she thought. Another woman would have understood immediately that no girl in her right mind would want to turn up at a hotel like the Ednam House looking anything less than her best.

'There's a very nice café just round the corner,' she suggested.

'I like the Ednam House,' he said, steering her firmly down the street. 'And you look fine to me.'

Actually, he thought she looked quite lovely. She was

wearing some sort of flowery dress that smelt of lavender and freshly laundered cotton, but it wasn't her dress that riveted his attention—it was her hair. Freed from its customary topknot, he could see that it was long—long and thick and riotously curly. There ought to be a law against covering hair like that with a nurse's cap, he decided. Hair like that was meant to be seen, to be touched, caressed.

Get a grip, Ben, he told himself, releasing her arm quickly. This woman's already in a relationship and you don't want to get involved with anyone again, not after Caroline.

'You know, I really would be quite happy to have lunch in one of the local cafés,' Izzie observed when they reached the wrought-iron gates that led into the Ednam House Hotel.

'Will you stop fussing about the way you look?' he demanded. 'I told you before that you look fine.' And without waiting for her reply, he strode through the hotel gates, across the gravel driveway and up the steps of the imposing Georgian hotel.

It was all very well for him, she thought with a deep sigh as she reluctantly followed him. In his pristine open-necked white shirt and elegant casual trousers he looked as though he'd just stepped out of the pages of some glossy hunting and fishing magazine, whereas she— She looked as though she should be going round to the tradesman's entrance for admittance.

It didn't take her long to discover, however, that she could have turned up wearing a potato sack for all the difference it would have made to the hotel staff. Ben had clearly been a very popular guest and any shortcomings she might have were very quickly overlooked in their obvious pleasure at seeing him again.

'Would you like to eat in the restaurant or the bar, Mr Farrell?' the manager asked, after greeting him like an old friend. 'Or perhaps you and your companion would prefer the terrace on such a beautiful day?'

Ben glanced across at Izzie questioningly.

'The terrace would be lovely,' she replied, and added in an undertone as they followed the manager outside, 'It will give me the chance to imagine I'm in one of those French towns you were talking about.'

'You're not going to let me forget that, are you?' Ben groaned.

'Of course I will,' she said impishly as they reached the terrace. 'But not until you've squirmed sufficiently.'

A burst of laughter came from him and she found herself smiling, too, as he pulled out a chair for her at one of the tables overlooking the River Tweed.

'I still think Steve could have taken some time off from his studying to help you with those groceries,' he observed as he sat down opposite her. 'They weigh a ton.'

Her smile faded. 'I think it might be better if we didn't talk about Steve, don't you?'

'But—'

'We'll only come to blows if we do,' she interrupted quickly, 'so let's talk about something else.'

'OK,' he replied, as the waiter handed them their menus. 'Why don't you tell me about yourself?'

'That should take all of five seconds,' she replied ruefully. 'I was born just outside Kelso, went to school in Kelso, did my training at the Kelso General—end of story.'

His lips quirked. 'I take it you like Kelso?'

'Like is an understatement. I love the town and its people. I love walking through the square, knowing that I'm treading in the footsteps of people like Bonnie Prince Charlie and Walter Scott. I love crossing the Horsemarket and imagining the Gipsies racing their horses over the cobbles, or standing in the square and picturing the hiring fairs of the last century.'

He smiled as he turned to the hovering waiter. 'I'll have the salmon salad, please. What about you, Izzie?'

'The same for me, thanks, but could I have a roll and butter as well?'

The waiter nodded and when he'd disappeared Ben turned back to her. 'So you're a romantic?'

'And how,' she exclaimed. 'Love at first sight and happy-ever-afters, old country cottages and schmaltzy music.' The smile on his face had died while she'd been speaking and she gazed at him curiously. 'I take it you're not a romantic?'

'Not any more, no.'

His voice had a bitter edge to it and she groaned inwardly. Of all the stupid things she could have said, that had to be the worst. Of course he wouldn't believe in happy-ever-afters, not when his wife had died so tragically.

Desperately she cast around in her mind for something to say, and eventually asked rather lamely, 'How are you settling in at Keeper's Cottage?'

He looked at her with surprise and then a slight smile appeared on his lips. 'Not a lot gets past the staff at the Kelso General, does it?'

'You'd better believe it.' She chuckled, relieved to see that his eyes were no longer dark. 'One sneeze and by the end of the day the entire staff will be offering you handkerchiefs and advice on cold cures.'

His smile widened. 'I like my cottage very much, thank you. The River Tweed virtually on my doorstep and the Eildon Hills to the west—what more could any man ask?'

'It's certainly a lovely house,' she murmured enviously.

'You know it?' he said as the waiter appeared with their salads.

She nodded. 'My biology teacher used to live there.'

He smiled but he didn't, she noticed, invite her to see what he'd done to the cottage.

'Just remember to be careful when you walk in the Eildons,' she observed as she lifted her knife and fork.

'Careful?' he repeated puzzled.

'Elves and fairies live there.'

'Oh, yes.' He laughed. 'And I was born yesterday.'

'I'm being serious,' she said solemnly, though her eyes danced. 'Thomas the Rhymer didn't believe in them either until the queen of the elves fell in love with him and spirited him away to her kingdom.'

A broad grin spread across his face. 'I can think of worse fates—particularly if the lady is beautiful.'

'Well, some say she is,' Izzie declared thoughtfully as she speared a piece of her salmon, 'but others say Thomas fell in love with her because of her hair—which I don't think can be right because people don't normally fall in love with someone because of their hair, do they?'

'They could.'

'But it's not very likely, is it?' she argued. 'I mean, you wouldn't fall in love with someone because of their hair, would you?'

'I might.'

She opened her mouth to protest, but he wasn't looking at her. His eyes were fixed on his meal, and her heart sank. She'd put her foot in it again. He'd told her that his wife had had lovely red hair. Why hadn't she remembered?

'Were you born in Newcastle?' she said in a desperate bid to change the conversation.

'I would have thought that was fairly obvious from my accent,' he observed with a slight smile, clearly just as relieved as she was to be talking about something else.

In truth it wasn't. Only when he was very angry—or deeply moved—could she hear the trace of Northumberland in his voice.

'My parents are both dead, and I've no brothers or sisters,' he continued as though in answer to her unspoken question, 'so there was nothing to keep me there.'

And no one to comfort you when your wife died, she thought sadly.

'I've got five brothers,' she declared.

'Five?' he echoed, his eyebrows shooting up.

'That's exactly how my poor mother felt.' She chuckled. 'She was so pleased when I finally came along but I was a cruel disappointment. She wanted to dress me in ribbons and lace, and I was far happier climbing trees with my brothers.'

'It must be nice, being part of a large family,' he observed.

'It can be a two-edged sword, believe me,' she replied with feeling, and he grinned.

'I bet your brothers gave all your boyfriends the third degree before they'd let them take you out.'

To his surprise her smile became slightly crooked. 'It wasn't exactly an onerous task for them—there weren't that many boyfriends.'

'Now, that I don't believe,' he exclaimed.

'It's true.' She sighed. 'Men aren't keen to date a girl who towers over them, and I was this height when I was fourteen.'

'You're not that tall,' he protested. 'In fact, you're quite a bit shorter than I am.'

'Yes, but you're the exception,' she argued. 'And it's not just my height, it's…' She frowned as she struggled to find the right words. 'I know I'm not pretty, but the trouble is I look so damn capable. If I get a puncture, men take one look at me and say, "Oh, she can manage," and drive straight past.'

He shook his head at her and smiled. 'All I can say is that the men in Kelso must be blind, or stupid, or both, if they don't think you're pretty.'

She didn't believe he meant it for a moment and so she laughed. 'Luckily for me, Steve is neither blind nor stupid.'

The smile on his lips hardened as he pushed his empty plate away from him. 'No, he's certainly not blind.'

Was it her imagination or had some of the warmth suddenly gone out of the day? They'd been getting on so well—in fact, she'd been amazed at how easy he'd been to talk to—and yet now he seemed irritated, almost angry.

'Ben—'

'Would you like a coffee?' he interrupted, beckoning to a waiter.

She glanced down at her watch and shook her head. 'I really must get my shopping home and it's already half past one.'

'You're sure?' he pressed.

'Absolutely positive,' she said regretfully, and then couldn't help adding, 'You see, my boss is a terrible stickler for punctuality, and he'll raise merry hell if I'm late.'

The hard look in his eyes vanished and he began to laugh. 'One day, Izzie Clark, one day—'

'You'll flatten me,' she broke in cheekily as he paid the bill. 'Yes, I know.'

She pushed back her chair to get to her feet, but he reached out a hand to prevent her.

'What is it?' she asked, sitting down again in panic. 'It's not a wasp, is it? I can't bear wasps.'

'It's not a wasp. It's just that you've got some little crumbs of bread stuck in the corner of your mouth.'

Embarrassed, she reached for a paper napkin only to see him lean forward and gently, very gently, run his thumb along her lower lip.

'Is that it now?' she said faintly, acutely aware that her heart had suddenly developed an erratic rhythm all of its own.

He shook his head.

'There's still one left in the corner,' he murmured, and as he ran his thumb along her lip again her heart rate went into overdrive.

He was too close to her, that was the trouble. Close enough for her to be able to smell a tantalising blend of pine soap and aftershave. Close enough for her to feel his breath warm against her throat. And close enough—way too close enough—for her to see the intriguing curl of dark hair at the top of his shirt and for her to wonder if it was actually as soft as it looked.

With a muttered exclamation she sprang to her feet, almost knocking over the carafe of water on the table in front of her in her haste to get away from him.

What in the world was happening to her? This was the second time he'd touched her, and the second time she'd experienced the same inexplicable reaction. If he'd been devastatingly handsome she might have understood it, but he wasn't. Yes, he had a nice mouth and an even nicer smile, and sometimes his eyes seemed so warm when he looked at her, but the world was full of men who could fit that description and she didn't feel like this when any one of them happened to touch her.

Uncomfortably she shot him a surreptitious glance. The one consoling thing was that he seemed totally unaware of the effect he had on her. His cheeks might be slightly flushed but, apart from that, he looked completely at ease whereas she... She shook her head as she followed him off the terrace, acutely conscious of having to force her legs to move. She didn't know why this kept happening, but it had to stop—and stop fast.

'Thanks for the lunch, and for the help with the shopping,' she said after he'd insisted on escorting her back to her car.

'Any time.' He smiled as he opened the door for her. 'And you were right—I really should go out more.'

Yes, but not with Joanna, she thought firmly. There had to be someone nice to whom she could introduce him, but oddly enough not one single suitable girl sprang to mind.

'Has Fran talked to you yet about the hospital fair next

week?' she asked, determinedly dragging her mind onto something else.

He shook his head. 'She probably knows I'm on duty that day.'

'You're not. We've all got the day off, apart from Tess and Steve.'

'All the more reason for me to keep myself available in case Steve needs me,' he replied.

'You've got a pager, remember,' she said, getting into her car. 'And as the fair is being held in the field across from the hospital you could easily get back to A and E if you were needed. And it's not as though Steve and Tess will be soldiering all alone in A and E,' she added as he opened his mouth, clearly intending to protest. 'Sister Norman and Staff Nurse Jenkins will be there.'

'But—'

'Don't "but" me,' she interrupted, her brown eyes dancing. 'Fran's the one you'll have to sweet-talk if you want to get out of it, but I warn you—she's pretty persistent.'

And she was. Fran waited until the steady stream of afternoon casualties had become a trickle before she approached Ben with a clipboard and a look of grim determination.

'But it's for such a good cause, Mr Farrell,' she said with an appealing smile as he began muttering something about other commitments. 'All the money raised at the fair and the dance in the evening goes to the hospital.'

'I know,' he replied as he erased the name of the last patient he had seen from the whiteboard, 'but I've never run a stall in my life—I wouldn't know how.'

'Why don't you give Mr Farrell the raffle tickets to sell?' Steve suggested. 'That's not a hard job.'

'No, but it's the most boring,' Izzie protested, overhearing him. 'We usually give it to one of the older groundsmen because it's not too tiring.'

Steve smiled. 'It was just a suggestion.'

And not a very nice one, Izzie thought with irritation as Fran leafed through the sheets of paper on her clipboard.

'If you're not keen on running a stall,' Fran continued with a frown, 'what about the five-a-side rugby? We're one short since the head of Physio put his back out.'

'I'm afraid I don't play rugby,' Ben said apologetically. 'Fishing and painting are my only hobbies.'

'Painting?' Steve repeated. 'As in flowers and birds and things?'

'More landscapes and portraits, actually.'

The curl of Steve's lip said exactly what he thought of that as an occupation.

'What about the derby, then?' Fran suggested, clearly determined not to be defeated.

'The derby?' Ben said.

'It's a race for white mice and people bet on the outcome. Mr Harvey normally runs it, but he's doing reconstructive surgery on that girl whose face got so badly smashed up in the car accident.'

'Do you think Mr Farrell will be able to get into Mr Harvey's clown costume?' Tess said, gazing up at Ben's huge frame dubiously.

'Clown costume?' Ben echoed, glancing from Tess to Fran in clear dismay.

'It isn't compulsory to dress up,' Fran declared, scowling at Tess. 'Most of us do to add to the fun of the occasion but you don't have to. So, will I put you down for the derby, Mr Farrell?'

'I don't know,' he replied uncertainly. 'I don't want to muck it up—'

'You wouldn't,' Fran insisted.

'If you're really not keen I could always swap shifts with you,' Steve said with a smile Izzie did not care for.

For a moment Ben said nothing and Izzie crossed her fingers behind her back. Please let him say yes to the stall, she prayed. He needed to start fitting in, and he never would if he kept a shield between himself and the rest of the team.

As though aware of her thoughts, Ben suddenly smiled. 'I'll take my chances with the white mice.'

'Great!' Fran beamed, making a note on her paper. 'And talking of offers,' she continued, 'Izzie, you're down for the white elephant stall this year, and I'm down for the tea tent…'

'And?' Izzie said with foreboding.

'Would you swop with me? I know it's a lot to ask,' Fran went on hurriedly as Izzie gazed at her in dismay, 'but Jim's got the day off and the white elephant stall always sells out fast so we could spend some time together.'

'Yes, but—'

'Please, Izzie. Jim and I have seen so little of each other recently, what with him doing nights with the fire service and me doing days at the hospital, and if I'm stuck in the tea tent I'll be lucky to see him at all. It's always bedlam in there.'

Don't I know it? Izzie groaned inwardly. The last thing she wanted was to be so exhausted by the end of the afternoon that she couldn't enjoy the dance that night—especially since that would be the only time she'd see Steve—but Fran's eyes were large and pleading, and with a sigh she found herself agreeing.

'Terrific,' Fran exclaimed. 'I'll make it up to you, I promise.'

Izzie couldn't think how, but she managed a weak smile.

'Right, if that's all sorted out, let's get back to work,' Ben declared. 'Steve and Izzie, there's a teenager in 3—name of Rachel Dalton—whose mother is a bit anxious about her. Fran, can you help me with the chest pains in 2, and, Tess, could you dress the bad gash in 6—I've done the stitching?'

'Jeez, did you hear the guy, Izzie?' Steve muttered as they made their way to cubicle 3. 'He paints!'

'So?' she replied evenly. 'Lots of people do.'

'Not the blokes I know,' he declared with derision.

'Look, just because he doesn't play rugby doesn't make him a wimp,' she declared with annoyance. 'You don't have to have your face and body battered to bits twice a week to prove you're a man.'

'OK, OK, keep your shirt on,' he protested. 'It was just an observation, that's all.'

She bit her lip as he pulled back the curtains around cubicle 3 to reveal a young teenager lying on the trolley, with her mother standing worriedly beside her. Why did she have to keep on fighting with him? It had never happened before, never.

'I'm probably just overreacting, Doctor,' Mrs Dalton said worriedly as soon as she saw them, 'but Rachel's always been so healthy, you see. Even as a child she didn't get any of the usual ailments, and when she became a teenager—'

'What exactly seems to be the problem, Mrs Dalton?' Steve interrupted gently.

'I—I'm sorry,' she stuttered, her cheeks reddening. 'I know I'm babbling…' She took a deep breath. 'Rachel had a bit of a headache on Monday and I gave her some aspirin which seemed to settle it, though she was a bit sick during the night. On Tuesday she came home from work saying she didn't feel at all well and I thought…well, I thought maybe she'd caught a cold. Though heaven alone knows how anyone could catch a cold in weather like this—'

'Did you take her temperature at all, Mrs Dalton?' Izzie asked, sensing Steve's growing impatience.

She nodded. 'It was up a little so I put her to bed. And then this morning… Her temperature's really gone up, and she seems sort of vague and confused.'

Steve uncurled his stethoscope. 'Could you take a deep breath for me, Rachel?'

The girl hardly seemed to hear him and her breathing was low and shallow.

'Pulse, Sister?' he asked as Izzie held Rachel's wrist and consulted her watch.

'Forty,' she murmured. 'And dropping.'

'How old is your daughter, Mrs Dalton?' Steve asked as he strapped the rubber cuff of the sphygmomanometer around Rachel's arm to take her blood pressure.

'Sixteen. She only started work this week at Belling's in town. I bought her the uniform and everything, and she seemed to be really enjoying it—'

'Have you noticed whether she's light-sensitive at all?' Steve broke in. 'I mean, does she seem to prefer to be in a darkened room?' he added as Mrs Dalton gazed at him blankly.

'Not that I've noticed, no.'

Izzie squinted over Steve's shoulder. The blood-pressure reading was so faint it was hardly registering. Steve glanced up at her and she knew what he was thinking—meningitis—and yet somewhere in the back of her mind a memory was stirring of a case she'd seen when she'd first started nursing.

'When did your daughter have her last period, Mrs Dalton?' she said quickly.

'W-what?' the woman stammered.

'Her period—when did she have her last one?'

'I...I don't know. Maybe a week ago, perhaps longer. She's sixteen, nurse—she doesn't tell me that sort of thing any more.'

'Of course not,' Izzie said soothingly as Steve gazed at her in confusion, 'but do you know whether she uses sanitary towels or tampons? It could be very important.'

Mrs Dalton frowned. 'Tampons—definitely tampons.'

'Could I have a word, Sister?' Steve asked. He waited only until they were outside the cubicle, before demanding

in an undertone, 'What are you playing at? Surely it's a
classic case of meningitis?'

'I'm not so sure,' she whispered back. 'It could be TSS—
toxic shock syndrome.'

'You think she's left a tampon in?'

'I don't know. I could be wrong, but the symptoms
would fit.'

'The trouble with TSS is that the symptoms are always
so damned vague,' he said ruefully. He frowned for a moment, then made up his mind. 'OK. Call Mr Brownlie in
Gynae and ask him to come down and take a look. If it is
toxic shock syndrome she needs treatment fast, and—'

'If it is meningitis she needs treatment quickly too,' Izzie
agreed.

'Well done, Dr Melville,' Mr Brownlie declared some time
later as Rachel was wheeled out of A and E on her way to
Intensive Care. 'It's not everyone who can recognise a case
of TSS.'

'I was just lucky,' Steve replied. 'At first I thought it was
meningitis.'

'It's easy to confuse the two.' Mr Brownlie nodded. 'In
fact, it's even easier not to pick it up at all. If only women
would use lower absorbency tampons, and alternate them
with an ordinary sanitary towel once in every twenty-four
hours—'

'And remember to remove the last tampon when their
periods are finished,' Izzie completed for him. 'Will she be
OK, do you think?'

'We've got a long way to go before we're out of the
woods, Sister, but at least Dr Melville's given her a fighting
chance.'

Izzie smiled and said nothing. She didn't mind Steve
taking the credit. Rachel could just as easily have been
suffering from meningitis, and perhaps praise from some-

one like Mr Brownlie was exactly what Steve needed to give him confidence for his exams.

'I owe you an apology, don't I?' Steve said as soon as they were alone.

'Of course you don't. It was just a lucky guess and—'

'I'm not talking about Rachel,' he cut in. 'I'm talking about me. I've been behaving like a real pig recently, haven't I?'

'You've not been your usual sunny self, no,' she said ruefully.

'It's these exams, Izzie.' He sighed. 'They're really getting me down but I know that's no excuse. Am I forgiven?'

She smiled. 'Of course you are. I just wish you and Ben—'

'Ben?'

Hot colour crept up the back of her neck as Steve's blue eyes grew cold.

'He asked me to call him that,' she said awkwardly. 'Look, I know you don't like him, but I think he's lonely.'

'Then let him buy a dog.'

An angry retort sprang to her lips and she crushed it down quickly. 'Steve, let's not fight about him. I hate fighting with you—we never did before.'

'I was never jealous before,' he observed.

'And you've no need to be now,' she protested.

He gazed at her searchingly for a moment, then reached out to caress the outline of her jaw with his fingertips. 'The trouble is I'm missing you so much. I was so desperate just to hear the sound of your voice this morning that I tried phoning you but all I got was your answering machine.'

'I was shopping.'

'But I phoned you at lunchtime, too, and you still weren't in.'

Uncomfortably she picked up the whiteboard eraser. Tell him you had lunch with Ben, her mind urged. It will be a whole lot worse if he finds out himself, but she couldn't.

He'd be angry—she knew he would—and she didn't want another row, not now when they were more at peace with each other.

'I had a snack in town,' she muttered.

He nodded and then sighed. 'I wish these exams were over, because when they are…' His blue eyes gleamed. 'When they are, I'm going to keep you in bed for a week to make up for all this deprivation!'

A bubble of laughter broke from her and as Steve leaned forward and kissed her lightly she didn't see the deep frown that appeared on Ben's face as he watched them from across the room.

He shouldn't have touched her this morning. The minute he'd done it he'd known it had been a big mistake. Just the feel of her moist lips beneath his fingers had been enough to send his pulses racing, and if he'd done what he'd really wanted—reached out and loosened her hair from its ponytail, fanned it out through his fingers…

Lord, but he must be going out of his mind, he decided as he felt his body reacting to the image he'd just conjured up in a way that it hadn't done for years. He'd always vowed that he'd never get involved with another woman, not after Caroline. But you can't get involved, can you? a little voice whispered at the back of his head. She isn't available, remember? But Steve Melville isn't good enough for her, he railed silently. He's going to hurt her, I know he is.

It's none of your business, the insidious little voice continued—*she's* none of your business—and as Izzie suddenly looked over her shoulder, clearly sensing his gaze on her, he turned abruptly on his heel and walked away.

CHAPTER FIVE

IZZIE squinted up at the cloudless blue sky. It was going to be another hot day. Just perfect, in fact, for the crowds who were already arriving for the Kelso General's annual August fair, but not so good for those who were going to be stuck in the refreshment tent all afternoon, serving teas and coffees.

'Izzie—Izzie, over here!'

Over the heads of those in front of her Izzie could see Fran waving to her from the bric-à-brac stall and grimly she strode towards her.

'I've got a bone to pick with you, Fran Walton!'

'Really?' the staff nurse queried, her face totally bland while her eyes sparkled. 'What about?'

'You know perfectly well what about,' Izzie replied severely. 'All that rubbish about wanting to swop jobs with me so that you could spend more time with Jim—'

'It was true, cross my heart,' Fran protested. 'I honestly didn't know what the tea girls were wearing this year. Mr Wakefield only came up with the idea three days ago.'

'So it's him I've got to thank, is it?' Izzie exploded. 'Wait till I get my hands on him. He'll be lucky if he can sit down for a week, far less examine his dratted blood samples!'

A whoop of laughter came from Fran. 'Give us a look at the costume, then,' she urged, and reached for Izzie's coat, only to watch her back away. 'Oh, come on. You're going to have to take your coat off eventually.'

'Eventually doesn't mean now,' Izzie replied firmly, and Fran laughed again.

'If you're looking for Mr Farrell,' she offered, seeing

Izzie's eyes drift towards the stalls in front of them, 'the committee put the derby beside the refreshment tent this year.'

'Who said I was looking for Mr Farrell?' Izzie demanded.

'Nobody,' Fran replied innocently as she adjusted her mop cap and smoothed down the sleeves of her Victorian-style cotton dress. 'It was just an observation, that's all.'

Izzie opened her mouth, then closed it again. She was in a no-win situation and she knew it, and with what she hoped was a dismissive toss of her head she walked away. Unfortunately it couldn't have been very convincing because she heard the sound of Fran's laughter following her.

So she was looking for Ben Farrell—so what? It was his first time at the fair and he was bound to be a little nervous. If she wanted to give him some moral support it was nobody's business but her own.

But it was easier said than done. No matter where she looked he wasn't to be seen. Fran had definitely said he'd be beside the refreshment tent but the only person there was some idiot dressed in a furry white mouse costume. Some very tall idiot dressed in a furry white mouse costume, she amended as she popped the toffee she'd sneaked from Deborah Grant's candy stall into her mouth.

'Care to try your luck in a game of chance, miss?' the giant mouse squeaked as he sidled up to her, clutching some tickets.

'Not just now, thanks,' she replied dismissively.

'It's for a very good cause,' the mouse persisted. 'All the money raised goes to the hospital.'

'I know it does, you idiot—I'm staff,' she retorted, only to hear a low deep chuckle that was oddly familiar. Her eyes flew up to the mouse's face and her jaw dropped. 'Ben...? Ben, is that you?'

'All present and correct, Sister Clark.' He grinned, tweaking his false nose and whiskers.

'But you look…you look…'

'Terrific, marvellous, wonderful?' he suggested.

'Ridiculous.' She burst out laughing. 'You look completely and utterly ridiculous.'

'And there was me thinking I looked the part,' he protested, sounding quite aggrieved.

She chuckled and shook her head. 'You're quite mad, you know. You're going to melt in that outfit today.'

'It's not too bad—I've got nothing on underneath it, you see.'

She choked as her toffee went down the wrong way and quickly he reached out to slap her on the back.

'Are you OK?' he said anxiously.

'Fine…just fine,' she spluttered. 'That'll teach me to steal something from one of the stalls.'

'I thought maybe I'd shocked you,' he said, his grey eyes dancing.

'Of course you haven't,' she said airily, annoyingly aware that her cheeks were red. 'Having nothing on under your suit… It's very sensible…very sensible indeed.'

And for some strange reason I'm going to have to spend the rest of the afternoon trying very hard not to think about it, she added mentally.

'What's your costume like?' he asked, his gaze sweeping over her. 'Or is that raincoat it?'

Her cheeks reddened still further. 'It's a sort of waitress-type thing,' she mumbled evasively.

'What sort of waitress-type thing?' he pressed. 'Come on, Izzie. You've seen how ridiculous I look. Let me see what you've got on.'

She stared at him uncertainly for a moment, then took a deep breath.

'OK,' she said as she began unbuttoning her coat, 'but I'm warning you. If you make one crack about the way I look, I swear I'll never speak to you again. Right,' she added, removing her coat. 'What do you think?'

He blinked as his eyes took in the frilly white apron and extremely low cut black dress which barely covered the tops of her breasts or her black-stockinged thighs. He blinked, but he didn't say a word.

'Well, say *something*, dammit,' she insisted, only just resisting the urge to duck behind the nearest stall and hide.

He opened his mouth and swallowed convulsively. 'For God's sake, put your coat back on, Izzie.'

In truth she'd been appalled when she'd seen herself in her mirror at home, but the discovery that he also felt she looked dreadful had her instantly bristling. 'Why?' she demanded. 'What's wrong with the way I look?'

'Good grief, girl, don't you realise you need a bodyguard dressed like that?' he exclaimed.

Her lips curved. 'You think I look OK, then?'

'OK?' he echoed. 'Izzie, take yourself off to the marquee while I can still keep my hands off you!'

She knew he didn't mean it—not really. He was just being kind but, bolstered by his words, she set off for the refreshment tent with a wide smile, certain she could face almost anything.

It took her only ten minutes of serving to realise it was darned near impossible, and after an hour she could have cheerfully strangled Fred Wakefield.

'I'm telling you this, Maureen,' she declared as she banged down a tray of dirty cups in front of the sister from Women's Surgical. 'If one more of these jokers pinches my bottom he's going to end up with a pot of coffee in his lap!'

Maureen grimaced expressively. 'I know how you feel, but you've got to admit it's a terrific money-making idea. The tea tent's never ever been this busy.'

'I'm not surprised,' Izzie protested. 'Every man's coming in to ogle us!'

'Ah, but they're having to pay for the privilege.' Maureen chuckled and then laughed out loud as Izzie scowled at her. 'Why don't you take a break? I don't think it's quite so busy now.'

Izzie gazed at her uncertainly. 'You're sure?'

'Go on—you've earned it.'

Izzie needed no second bidding. She was out of the refreshment tent in seconds and her eyes went automatically to the derby stall.

The good news was that Ben seemed to be enjoying himself. The bad news was that he wasn't alone. Joanna was with him, stunningly dressed in a safari suit of beige linen, and she couldn't have got any closer to him if she'd actually climbed inside his costume.

It's none of your business, a little voice whispered as she walked towards them. Maybe he likes women hanging around his neck, whispering sweet nothings in his ear. I don't care if he does, she told the little voice. The last woman I want to see doing that is Joanna Ogilvy.

'Good heavens, Izzie, what on earth have you got on?' Joanna asked as soon as she saw her.

'Isn't it obvious?' she replied as evenly as she could. 'It's a waitress outfit.'

'Well, I've got to admire you,' Joanna said, her green eyes brimming with laughter. 'It's not every girl who doesn't mind looking ridiculous.'

And it's not every girl who's such an out and out bitch Izzie thought, glancing quickly across at Ben.

Was it wishful thinking on her part or did he look relieved to see her? Of course it was wishful thinking. No red-blooded male could possibly want to be rescued from someone like Joanna. She was probably as welcome as a plague of midges in a nudist colony.

'Oh, please, don't run away on my account,' Joanna observed sweetly, clearly reading her mind. 'I'm just leaving but I'll see you tonight, Ben.'

'Tonight?' Izzie repeated, turning to Ben, her eyebrows raised, as Joanna disappeared into the crowd.

He pulled back the head of his costume and ran a hand through his damp hair. 'She's going to the dance after the fair.'

'Is she?' Izzie said with as much indifference as she could manage, but found herself adding waspishly, 'Her ankle seems to have made a miraculous recovery.'

'Doesn't it?'

His face was totally bland but there was a smile tugging at the corners of his lips and she decided it might be wise to change the subject.

'How's the derby been going?'

'Really well.'

'No regrets about deciding to take part, then?'

'None at all.'

Absently she adjusted one of the flags on the wooden racetrack. There didn't seem to be a whole lot left to say and, feeling oddly deflated, she turned to go.

'Are you on your break?' he asked quickly, and when she nodded he waved to Deborah Grant on the candy stall. 'Keep an eye on my mice for a little while, will you, Deborah?'

'I don't think she actually said yes,' Izzie pointed out as Ben began steering her through the throng with the clear sound of Deborah's protesting voice ringing out behind them.

'Of course she did.' He grinned, taking off his false nose and whiskers. 'So, what'll it be—tea or coffee?'

'You've got to be joking,' she groaned. 'I've seen enough of both to last me a lifetime. What I'd like is an ice cream.'

'Your wish is my command,' he said with a laugh.

The queue at the ice-cream stall was huge, but Ben shamelessly pulled rank and Izzie was still chuckling when they sat down to enjoy their ices in a quiet corner of the field.

'Of all things to tell people—that you were head of A

and E and I was suffering from a bad attack of caffeine tannic!'

'Well, you are, aren't you?' he replied, and as she laughed again he gazed out at the milling crowd. 'You were right about everyone turning up to support the hospital. I even saw that little old lady who used to haunt A and E, but she ran away before I could apologise to her.'

Izzie wiped her sticky fingers on her handkerchief and sighed. 'I'm afraid Mavis is a law unto herself. If she doesn't want to talk to you, she won't.'

'What do you know about her?' he asked curiously, watching her pinning back a stray tendril of hair that had managed to escape from her top knot.

'Nothing, and that's the way Mavis seems to like it.'

'Interesting,' he murmured.

'But not as interesting as Joanna Ogilvy?' she suggested, shooting him a sly, sideways glance.

He smiled. 'You're fishing, Izzie.'

'Sorry,' she said, and then swore as the recalcitrant tendril descended onto her shoulders again.

'Here, let me do that,' he offered.

Obediently she handed him the hairclip.

'If it will set your mind at rest,' he continued as she turned her head so that he could reach the back of her hair, 'I won't ever marry again.'

Try telling that to Joanna, she thought acidly, and then shivered as his fingers brushed the nape of her neck.

'Am I hurting you?' he asked, concern plain in his voice.

'Your…your hands are a bit cold, that's all,' she lied. 'But you know what they say. Cold hands—'

'Warm heart,' he finished for her, his voice unexpectedly husky against her ear.

It was happening again, she thought with dismay. Her heart rate was accelerating alarmingly again, and this time she could also feel a dull throbbing heat spreading from the pit of her stomach down into her thighs.

Stop it, Izzie, she told herself, just stop it. The next thing you know you'll be fantasising about Fred Wakefield and then you really will be carted away to the psychiatric ward.

'I really should be getting back to the tea tent,' she said through lips which had suddenly become dry. 'Maureen must be thinking I've deserted her, and there're only six of us serving, and—'

'Izzie.'

His hands had come to rest on her shoulders, and her stomach tightened.

'Yes?' she said faintly.

'Look at me.'

She didn't want to. She didn't want to turn round and face him, but she did.

A gentle smile was curving his lips, and she tried to smile back, but the corners of her mouth wobbled precariously. 'Ben…'

Without a word he leaned forward and cupped her face in his large hands. Surely he wasn't going to kiss her. Surely he wasn't, but he did.

Never had she been kissed so gently before, and yet the gentleness was in no way tentative. It was the gentleness of a strong man who was holding himself in check, and as tiny shivers of pleasure ran down her spine she knew she wanted to taste that power, experience it.

Instinctively her lips parted under his and for a second—one tantalising, wonderful second—he deepened the kiss, sliding his tongue gently into her mouth, and then they both sprang guiltily apart as a female voice declared, 'I *thought* it was you!'

'M-Mrs Dalton,' Izzie stammered, gazing up red-cheeked at the woman beaming down at them. 'How…how nice to see you again.'

'And you too, Nurse,' Mrs Dalton replied with a cursory nod at Ben. 'I was hoping to see that nice young doctor again—the one who treated my Rachel. She's just been moved out of Intensive Care, you see, and I wanted to thank him for all he did.'

'I'm afraid Dr Melville's not here today,' Izzie replied, pulling herself together quickly, 'but I'll certainly pass on your thanks to him.'

'I'd be very grateful if you would, Nurse, though, as I recall, you were the one who first asked about her periods and whether she used tampons—'

'It's really lovely to see you again, Mrs Dalton,' Izzie interrupted hurriedly. 'I hope you have a wonderful day at the fair.'

'I will now that I know my Rachel is on the mend.' The woman beamed. 'And thank you again, Nurse. I can't tell you how grateful I am.'

Izzie bit her lip as Rachel's mother walked away. It hadn't just been Mr Brownlie who'd congratulated Steve on spotting Rachel's TSS. Ben had praised him, too, and now he was going to be furious at the deception. Unhappily she pulled at the blades of grass beside her, waiting for the explosion to come, but nothing happened. Was he speechless with anger? she wondered, hesitantly lifting her head to look at him, only to see that he didn't look angry. He looked uncomfortable and embarrassed.

'Izzie, that was a mistake.'

She didn't need her nursing diploma to tell her that he wasn't talking about Steve. And he was right, she told herself. Their kiss had been a mistake. She and Ben Farrell. They were like chalk and cheese, oil and water, and yet…and yet…

He was gazing at her anxiously and she managed to dredge up a smile. 'You don't have to apologise, Ben. We're friends, remember, and what's the harm in a kiss between friends?'

Was that relief or disappointment she saw in his eyes? She couldn't be sure, but there was no mistaking the speed with which he got to his feet when the shrill sound of his pager suddenly rent the air.

'There must be trouble in A and E,' he observed. 'Would you tell Deborah that I don't know when—or if—I'll be back?'

'We'll get someone else to tell her,' she said firmly. 'I'm coming with you.'

'But—'

'I'm never going to get a better excuse to escape from the tea tent, am I?' she pointed out, and was relieved to see his expression lighten.

If her appearance had caused comment in the tea tent, it was nothing compared to the reactions of the porters and paramedics when they reached the hospital.

'Hey, Izzie, you can take my pulse any day of the week if you promise to wear that outfit!'

'Whoa, Sister, I'm feeling a little faint—how about some mouth-to-mouth resuscitation?'

'Simmer down, boys,' Ben ordered, his lips quirking. 'Have you never seen a waitress outfit before?'

'Yes, but not quite so much of the waitress!' someone shouted. 'You'd better be careful, too, Doc—the hospital cat's loose!'

'Do you reckon we're ever going to live this down?' Ben muttered, crimson-cheeked, as they walked smartly through the doors of A and E.

'You might, but I doubt if I ever will,' she groaned, equally flushed.

'I did warn you, didn't I?' He grinned. 'That outfit of yours should be X-rated.'

She chuckled and blushed even more.

'Tell Steve I'll be with him in a minute,' he continued as they passed through Reception to a collection of giggles and whispered comments. 'I've just got to collect my white coat.'

Izzie wished she had a white coat to hide under when

she walked into the treatment room and saw Steve's blue eyes widen.

'Ye gods,' he exclaimed. 'You haven't been walking around dressed like that all afternoon, have you?'

'And what if I have?' she said defensively.

A burst of laughter came from him. 'You'll do anything for a laugh, won't you, babe?'

'A laugh?' she repeated.

'Oh, sweetie, much as I love you, you're not really the *femme fatale* type, are you?'

She blinked quickly, uncomfortably aware that she was close to tears. Had people been laughing at her all afternoon? Had Ben simply been making a joke at her expense? It was a horrible feeling.

'OK, what have we got?' Ben asked as he strode in, his mouse costume barely covered by his white coat.

Steve stared at him, transfixed, for a second, then pulled himself together. 'A teenager who's OD'd in cubicle 1, a man who's lopped off three of his toes with a chainsaw in 2, a woman with a possible perforated appendix in 3, a drunk with the DTs in 4 and a farmer and his son with multiple injuries are on their way by ambulance.'

'OK,' Ben declared. 'The patient with delirium tremens—is he having convulsions?'

'Just the shakes and hallucinations.'

'Get him a bed in ward 5.'

'They won't like it.'

'Tough,' Ben snapped. 'The woman in 3—why do you think she's got a perforated appendix?'

'The severe abdominal pain she had in the lower right-hand side of her abdomen seems to have disappeared, but she's feverish and her stomach is quite tender.'

Ben frowned. 'OK, phone Theatre and tell them she's on her way. What about the chainsaw case—have we got his toes?'

Steve nodded. 'His wife brought them in. She'd packed

them round with ice from the freezer. And before you ask,'
he continued as Ben opened his mouth, 'the ice was
wrapped in a pillowcase so there's no danger of freezer
burns.'

'Great. Contact Ed Harvey and tell him we need his expertise. That leaves us with the OD and the farmer and his
son. Any idea what the teenager's OD'd on?'

'Paracetamol,' Steve replied. 'Taken an hour ago so the
pills should still be in her stomach.'

'Any word of the injuries to the farmer and his son?'
Ben asked.

'According to the report, the father has a broken leg and
crushed ribs, and the son has possible internal bleeding.
Apparently their tractor rolled, trapping them both inside
the cabin.'

'How old is the son?'

'Three.'

'*Three?*' Ben gasped. 'What the hell was a child that age
doing in a tractor?'

'I'm afraid it's pretty common practice round here.'
Steve sighed. 'Dads like to give their sons their first taste
of farming at an early age.'

'Even though it might turn out to be their last taste of
anything,' Ben commented grimly 'Did you page
Paediatrics?'

'I thought you might want to see the child first.'

'Well, in future I'd be obliged if you didn't think,' Ben
flared. 'You should have paged them immediately. Go and
do it now, instead of wasting even more valuable time!'

Steve flushed to the roots of his blond hair and went.

'Is there anything I can do to help?' Izzie asked, her
voice tight.

'You can help Staff Nurse Jenkins administer a gastric
lavage on the OD case.'

'Fine,' she said, her voice even tighter.

Quickly she began walking down the treatment room, only to find her arm caught.

'Izzie, I'm sorry,' Ben murmured. 'I didn't mean to sound so brusque—'

'I don't think I'm the one you should be apologising to, do you?' she interrupted.

He let go of her arm and his jaw hardened. 'Izzie, he should have known to phone Paediatrics. He's an SHO, for God's sake, not a second-year medical student!'

He was right, she knew he was, but there was no way she was going to agree with him, and without a word she strode swiftly into cubicle 1.

Had he been laughing at her all afternoon? she wondered as she and Jenny Jenkins explained to the frightened teenager what a gastric lavage entailed. Surely he couldn't be so cruel? But maybe he hadn't thought he was being cruel. Perhaps, like Steve, he'd merely thought she was the kind of girl who didn't mind looking stupid.

But he kissed you, her mind whispered as she and Jenny began passing a lubricated tube down through the girl's mouth into her stomach. Yes, but he told you afterwards that it had been a mistake.

Angrily she crushed down a small sob lodged in her throat as she began to pour water through the funnel at the end of the tube into the girl's stomach. Get a grip, Izzie, she told herself. The Kelso General thrives on gossip and Jenny's already looking at you oddly. The last thing you want is the whole hospital speculating about you and Ben. And what's there to speculate about, anyway? It was just a kiss—it meant nothing to Ben or to you.

Eventually, and after what seemed like an eternity, the contents of the girl's stomach began to run clear and, leaving Jenny to pass a slick of charcoal down the tube to absorb any remaining paracetamol, Izzie wearily left the cubicle. It would be at least five days before they'd know whether the teenager had done her liver permanent damage or not but for the moment all they could do was wait.

'You look exhausted.'

'So do you,' she observed, turning to see Ben sitting on the end of one of the trolleys, his mouse costume spattered with traces of blood. 'How are the farmer and his son?'

'We lost the child.'

'Oh, Ben, I'm sorry—'

'It's almost five o'clock,' he interrupted, obviously not wanting to talk about it. 'I don't think it's worth our while going back to the fair now, do you?'

She shook her head.

'Time to go home, then,' he continued, and started to lead the way out of the hospital and across to the car park.

She nodded and he shot her a thoughtful glance.

'Are you still cross with me because of what I said to Steve?'

She took a deep breath and gathered the courage to look him in the face. 'Ben, do I...do you think I look silly in this outfit?'

'Silly?' he echoed, coming to a halt.

'Stupid, ridiculous?'

His eyes narrowed. 'You're thinking about what Joanna said, aren't you? Oh, Izzie—'

'Tell me the truth, Ben,' she interrupted. 'When you look at me, do you...do you feel like laughing?'

'Laughing?' he exclaimed, his voice suddenly harsh. 'That's the last thing I feel like doing, believe me.'

'You mean it?' she said uncertainly. 'I don't look—?'

'Izzie...you look wonderful.'

To her dismay, tears welled in her eyes, and she blinked rapidly. 'Thank you. I don't care if you're lying or not. Thank you.'

He gazed at her wordlessly for a moment, then shook his head. 'Why do you have so little confidence in yourself?'

She intended to protest, to say he was wrong, and yet

she heard herself replying, 'I guess it's because of the way I look.'

'What's wrong with the way you look?' he demanded.

'I'm too damn big, Ben,' she exclaimed miserably. 'All the jibes I used to get when I was growing up—"Is it cold up there?", "Do you have to duck every time you go through a door?". I laughed them off, but they hurt. And, to cap it all, I'm not exactly what you'd call willowy either.'

'I'd say you were just about perfect. Proportion-wise, that is,' he added quickly as her head came round in surprise.

'Really?' she said, despising herself for fishing for a compliment yet longing to hear it from him nevertheless.

'Really.'

His eyes were warm, his smile was gentle, and an answering smile curved her own lips. 'You know, I think that's the nicest thing anyone's ever said to me.'

'Izzie—'

'Though, to be fair,' she couldn't help but add, 'Steve sometimes comes up with some pretty nice compliments, too.'

The smile on his lips disappeared. 'Does he?'

She'd angered him. She didn't know how, or why, but she had, and tentatively she touched his arm. 'Ben—'

'I've got to go,' he interrupted brusquely. 'I'll see you tomorrow.'

She nodded, but as he began to walk towards his car she suddenly remembered. 'Tomorrow?' she called after him. 'But surely I'll see you at the dance tonight, won't I?'

He shook his head. 'I'm going to give it a miss.'

'But you can't!' she protested, only to redden when he gazed at her with surprise. 'I mean, Joanna...she'll be so disappointed.'

'I expect she'll live,' he said drily.

'Please, come,' she urged. 'Look on it as a form of occupational therapy—getting out, meeting new people.'

For a long moment he said nothing and then he sighed. 'OK, but, I warn you, I'm not much of a dancer.'

He'd been lying, Izzie thought as she sat at a table in the refreshment tent that evening and watched him whirl past with yet another partner in his arms. He was a very good dancer, and a dedicated one, too.

Since he'd arrived he'd danced with virtually every unattached woman in the room. Damn it, he'd even danced with the canteen cook, and yet still he hadn't asked her to dance. But surely you don't want to dance with him? her heart said. You know what always happens when he touches you. All the more reason why I should dance with him, she answered back firmly. It's time I got over it.

But it didn't look as though she'd get the chance to. He hadn't so much as glanced in her direction all evening, far less spoken to her, and yet he'd danced with Joanna three times. Not that she was counting, of course, but it was very difficult not to notice Joanna in that dress—that dress made of pale green silk, with a fitted beaded bodice, tiny shoulder straps and a skirt that billowed out like a dream.

'Having fun?' Fran asked as she sat down beside her.

'Lovely, thanks,' Izzie replied with a cheerfulness she was very far from feeling.

And she supposed she should have been enjoying herself. She hadn't lacked partners all night but somehow being steered slowly round the dance floor by Fred Wakefield from Haematology and then having her toes crushed by Mr Dickinson from Paediatrics came a very poor second to being whirled elegantly around the room by Ben Farrell.

'No sign of Steve yet?' Fran asked, seeing Izzie turn eagerly in her seat as a crowd of latecomers arrived.

'He wasn't due to get off duty until nine,' Izzie replied, subsiding into her seat again with a faint sigh. 'And you

know what he's like—he's probably got talking to someone.'

Fran glanced at her watch. It was eleven-thirty.

'That girl Mr Farrell's talking to,' Fran said. 'Isn't she
the one—'

'Who caused all the fuss in A and E?' Izzie finished for
her. 'Yes, she is.'

'Well, she may be a pain, but her dress is gorgeous,'
Fran said enviously. 'It must have cost a small fortune.'

It did, but that still hadn't stopped Izzie from going back
to the shop late last night, determined to buy it at all costs,
only to discover it had already been sold. Morosely she
stared down at her blue satin dress with the heart-shaped
neckline—the dress she'd worn to every hospital dance
since she'd joined the staff. Nobody in their right mind
would ever describe it as gorgeous.

'Oh, look,' Fran continued, her eyes lighting up. 'Mr
Farrell's coming over. Maybe he's going to ask you to
dance?'

'I don't care if he does or not,' Izzie said airily, and knew
that Fran wasn't for one moment deceived.

But he didn't ask her to dance. He simply sat down at
the table and smiled at them both.

'I'd no idea you were such a keen dancer, Mr Farrell,'
Fran observed.

'I'm not,' he replied, 'but my occupational therapist ad-
vised me to make an effort and so I have.'

'Your occupational therapist?' she repeated blankly.

He nodded, his face carefully expressionless. 'One very
persuasive lady, believe me.'

A choke of laughter came from Izzie, and Fran glanced
across at her questioningly then cleared her throat.

'Izzie's a very good dancer. In fact,' she continued,
deftly avoiding the kick that had been aimed at her under
the table, 'the band are just beginning to play one of her
favourite waltzes now.'

Fran was about as subtle as a sledgehammer, Izzie thought with dismay as Ben got reluctantly to his feet. He obviously didn't want to dance with her. In fact, he looked as though open-heart surgery would have been infinitely preferable, but under Fran's pointed gaze there was nothing he could do but lead her out onto the dance floor.

And as soon as he took her in his arms she knew it was going to be a nightmare. Where, oh, where was the laughing man who'd whirled so many women around the floor, looking as though both he, and they, were having a wonderful time? Where was the man who'd kissed her so tenderly and unforgettably this afternoon? He never looked at her, he didn't talk to her, and he couldn't have held her at greater arm's length if he'd tried.

'Ben, is there something wrong?' she asked eventually.

'No.'

'Are you angry with me?' she pressed. 'Have I said something—done something—?'

'Izzie, there's nothing wrong!' he exclaimed, his voice tight.

They'd stopped dancing and she knew people must be staring at them but she didn't care. All she could see was Ben's face, his features unexpectedly harsh in the dim light from the swinging lanterns.

'There must be something,' she insisted. 'I thought we were friends, and yet tonight… Ben, if I've offended you in some way, you must know I wouldn't do it deliberately.'

'Izzie, it isn't you or anything you've done,' he murmured.

'Then what is it?' she asked, confusion and hurt plain on her face.

'Izzie…' Gently he reached out and touched her cheek with his fingers. 'Isabella, it's me.'

'You?' she said, bewildered. 'I'm sorry but I don't understand—'

'And that's exactly how I want to keep it,' he said shortly.

'But, Ben—'

Something behind her caught his attention and he stiffened. 'Steve's arrived.'

She didn't even look round. 'Ben, please—'

'Fran was right—you're a very good dancer,' he said with an uneven smile that somehow seemed to tear at her heart before he turned abruptly on his heel and walked away, leaving her staring blindly after him.

CHAPTER SIX

'WHAT seems to be the trouble, Mrs Lawson?' Ben asked as he pulled back the curtains around cubicle 3 to reveal a stout woman in her mid-fifties perched precariously on the end of the trolley.

'It's my ankle, Doctor,' she boomed in a voice that could have deputised for a foghorn. 'I stove it a couple of days ago and as you can see…'

'It's very badly swollen.' He nodded.

'I was going to leave it until I go back down south at the end of the week,' the woman continued as Ben gently prodded round her ankle, 'but my hubby insisted that—'

'How long have you had this?' Ben interrupted, pointing to a small circle of inflamed skin halfway up Mrs Lawson's calf.

She peered down at it and frowned. 'A couple of weeks—maybe a month. As I was saying, I wouldn't have bothered you, but my hubby—'

'Have you been experiencing any flu-like symptoms lately?' Ben continued, his eyes fixed thoughtfully on her leg.

'As a matter of fact I have, but—'

'Could you unbutton your blouse for me, please?'

'My blouse?' she repeated as he unrolled his stethoscope. 'But I came in about—'

'Your blouse, please, Mrs Lawson.'

Mrs Lawson gazed across at Izzie in confusion but she couldn't help her. She didn't have the faintest idea where Ben's line of questioning was going either, and with a deep sigh Mrs Lawson did as he'd asked.

'Have you noticed any pain in your joints recently?' Ben

murmured as Mrs Lawson reluctantly breathed in and out for him.

'No, I haven't,' she retorted. 'The only pain I've got is in my ankle.'

'Your chest sounds are quite clear,' he observed, 'and your heart rhythm's excellent, but I'd like to take a blood sample—'

'I'm sure you would, but you're not going to,' Mrs Lawson interrupted with asperity as she began rebuttoning her blouse. 'I came in about my ankle, Doctor, not to have my chest examined or to have blood samples taken.'

Ben pocketed his stethoscope. 'Mrs Lawson, you've definitely stoved your ankle, and rest will take care of that, but I think you've also been bitten by a tick—in particular, an *Ixodes ricinus*, or deer tick.'

'People get bitten by ticks all the time,' she replied dismissively. 'It's one of the hazards of being in the country.'

'A deer tick is rather different, I'm afraid,' he said gently. 'They carry Lyme disease and that red circle on your leg is one of the classic symptoms—as, indeed, were the flu-like symptoms you experienced. I need a blood sample from you to confirm it, but I'm pretty certain that's what you've got.'

Mrs Lawson gazed at him silently for a moment. 'This Lyme disease. It's serious, isn't it?'

'Luckily I think we've caught it in time, and it can be cured by antibiotics.'

'You didn't answer my question, Doctor,' Mrs Lawson pressed. 'If my hubby hadn't nagged me into coming in, what could have happened?'

'The consequences could have been very serious indeed,' Ben admitted. 'Left untreated, the disease would have caused extensive arthritis in your joints and eventually cardiac and neurological disorders.'

Mrs Lawson shook her head in disbelief. 'All that from one tiny little bite?'

He nodded and took the syringe Izzie was holding out to him. 'In future I'd suggest you always wear trousers when you're walking in the woods. And make sure that the bottoms of your trousers are tight against your ankles.'

'You bet your life I will,' Mrs Lawson said fervently.

Quickly he took the sample and Izzie despatched it to the lab with a request for it to be tested immediately. With Lyme disease, the sooner it was diagnosed and treated the better.

'How on earth did he recognise it?' Fran asked some time later when Ben's diagnosis had been confirmed. 'I've only ever seen one case before and that was in a forestry worker.'

'Was it?' Izzie murmured, her eyes fixed on Ben as he stood talking to Tess.

Fran followed the direction of her gaze and then cleared her throat awkwardly. 'Izzie, I'm not being nosy or anything, but are you OK?'

'OK?' she echoed in surprise. 'Of course I'm OK.'

'Then how come you're as bright as a button one minute and then down in the dumps the next?'

Izzie opened her mouth to protest and then closed it again. Fran was right. Ever since the day of the August fair she'd been as moody as hell and she couldn't for the life of her think why.

Fran picked up a box of dressings and examined it with apparent interest. 'I wondered if it had anything to do with Mr Farrell?' she said casually.

'Mr Farrell?' Izzie said, annoyingly aware that a wash of colour was creeping across her cheeks. 'Why on earth should my behaviour have anything to do with him?'

'Well, I did hear that he's been seeing a lot of that Joanna Ogilvy lately.'

'So?' Izzie flared. 'He's single, unattached and over eighteen, isn't he? Good grief, Fran, anyone would think you were suggesting I had a special interest in the man. He's my boss, that's all. I'm in love with Steve, remember.'

Fran gazed at her thoughtfully. 'Are you?'

'Of course I am,' Izzie exclaimed. 'What girl with half a brain wouldn't be? He's handsome, charming, good company—'

'When he wants to be,' Fran muttered under her breath, but Izzie heard her.

'And what's that supposed to mean?' she demanded angrily.

Fran sighed as she put down the box of dressings. 'Nothing—nothing at all. Forget I said anything. It's none of my business.'

'Too right it's not!' Izzie retorted.

And it wasn't any of her business, Izzie thought furiously as Fran stared up at her for a moment, her face hurt, before turning on her heel and walking away.

OK, so maybe she and Steve had been doing a lot of arguing lately, but for Fran to imply that she was interested in Ben Farrell...

So you don't care about him dating Joanna? a small voice asked at the back of her mind. Of course I care, she replied. I care because it's beyond me how such an intelligent man can have such rotten taste.

What's wrong with his taste? the little voice demanded. She's petite and beautiful and sophisticated. She's also a complete bitch, Izzie thought waspishly. And what does that make you for thinking it? the little voice asked laughingly.

Angrily she picked up the box of dressings Fran had discarded. No wonder she felt edgy all the time. The man she loved was behaving like a bear with a sore head, and the man she'd grown to like and respect was leaving himself wide open to being hurt.

It's none of your business if he gets hurt, the little voice pointed out. Even if he decided he wanted to marry a serial bigamist, it would still be none of your business. Oh, shut up, she told the annoying little voice, and walked crossly down the treatment room.

It was a long and weary day. It wasn't helped, of course, by the fact that every time Izzie looked up she found Fran's eyes on her, her face troubled. Well, if she expected her to forgive her for her remark about Steve she was going to have to wait a long time, Izzie thought vexedly. They might be friends, but there were limits, and interfering in her private life was one of them.

'God, Izzie, you're about as much fun these days as a wet weekend,' Steve said after they'd eaten a largely silent lunch in the canteen together. 'What's the matter with you?'

'I'm just feeling a bit down, that's all,' she said as they made their way back to A and E.

'Down?' he exploded. 'Sweetie, if anyone's got a right to feel down it's me. I'm the one sitting exams this weekend. I'm the one who's been working all day and studying all night for the last six weeks.'

'Well, pardon me for complaining,' she retorted. 'I didn't realise you'd cornered the monopoly on feeling miserable. I didn't realise only you were allowed to feel—'

'OK, OK,' he interrupted, holding up his hands defensively. 'You've made your point. Let's just forget it, shall we?'

She didn't want to forget it. Right now she wanted nothing better than a really good argument with someone, but one look at Steve's set face told her that he might not be a wise choice.

What was wrong with her? she wondered as she followed him into the treatment room. Why did she feel so out of sorts and unhappy? It didn't make sense. She had everything she'd ever wanted—a handsome man who loved her, a good job, excellent colleagues—so why did she feel as she did?

'Anything for us, Tess?' Steve asked as soon as he saw her.

'Well, there's a Mr Gardner in 1, complaining of a severe headache.'

Quickly Steve pulled back the curtains round the cubicle, and a wide smile of delight lit up his face as he gazed down at the young man lying on the trolley. 'Hey, it's Donald Gardner, isn't it? Lock forward for the local rugby team?'

The young man nodded weakly.

'I used to play a bit myself at university,' Steve observed. 'I wasn't in your class, of course, and I was a winger, but I was quite good, if I say so myself. So, what's the problem?'

'It's not really a problem as such,' Donald replied, heaving his massive frame upright with difficulty. 'It's just I've got this headache and I can't seem to shift it.'

'Were you playing yesterday?' Steve asked as he sounded Donald's chest.

'In the afternoon against Melrose.'

'And were you knocked out at all?' Steve murmured as he shone his ophthalmoscope into Donald's eyes.

'I don't think so… To tell you the truth, Doctor, I don't really remember very much about yesterday apart from the fact that we won.'

'So it was celebrations all round last night, was it?' Steve laughed. 'It sounds to me like you've got the mother and father of all hangovers. A couple of aspirin and a good night's sleep should do the trick.'

And with a wide smile he was gone.

'Is there someone waiting for you in Reception, Mr Gardner?' Izzie asked with concern as the young man struggled unsteadily to his feet.

'Waiting for me?' he said blankly.

'How did you get here? Did someone drive you in?'

'I think…' He smiled and shook his head. 'God, I don't

know where my brains are today, Nurse. The wife, yes, it was the wife who brought me in.'

Quickly Izzie took his wrist in her hand and felt for his pulse. 'Do you feel drowsy at all, Mr Gardner?'

'A bit but, then, I didn't get much sleep last night. This headache, you see—'

'How about your arms and legs?' she interrupted. 'Do they feel numb?'

He gazed at her blankly. 'To be perfectly honest, Nurse, I don't really feel them that much at all.'

Gently Izzie pushed him back onto the trolley. 'Would you wait there for just a minute?'

'Wait?' he echoed. 'But the doctor said—'

'I'll be back in a minute,' Izzie smiled reassuringly, and went quickly through the cubicle curtains.

Steve listened to her misgivings in total silence and then shook his head. 'Izzie, you know what these rugby teams are like. They play hard and they drink hard. All he needs is to lay off the booze for a bit and a few nights' sleep.'

'You don't think that maybe you should arrange for him to have an X-ray?'

'Look, who's the doctor here—you or me?' he snapped. 'But—'

'But nothing, Izzie. Discharge the guy.'

She opened her mouth then closed it again tightly. As he'd said, he was the doctor, not her, and she had no right to query his diagnosis.

Slowly she began to walk back down to the cubicle. Today was turning out to be a really rotten day, and she still had four hours of her shift to go.

'Something bothering you, Izzie?' Ben asked as she walked past him without a word.

'No, nothing,' she began, then stopped. What if it wasn't nothing? What if there really was something seriously wrong with Donald Gardner? Ben was gazing encouragingly at her and she took a deep breath. 'It's the patient in

1. Steve thinks he's simply suffering from a hangover but...'

'But?' he prompted.

She could feel her cheeks reddening. It was now or never, and she knew it. 'Would you take a look at him?' she asked, her words coming out in a rush.

For a moment he said nothing. For an even longer moment she thought he was going to refuse, then without a word he turned on his heel and strode down the treatment room into cubicle 1.

'Tess, what are you doing right now?' she asked as the student nurse appeared with some dressings.

'Steve's just finished stitching the hand of that girl from the butcher's shop and I'm going to bandage it.'

'I'll do the bandaging. You help Mr Farrell with Donald Gardner.'

'Donald Gardner?' Tess said in surprise. 'But I thought Steve had already—'

'Just do it, Tess,' Izzie said firmly.

The student nurse gazed at her curiously for a moment, then hurried away quickly and Izzie sighed with relief. It was bad enough that she'd asked Ben to give a second opinion but to stand there and watch him do it... Make me wrong, she prayed. I'd far rather look stupid and overcautious than be right.

It was almost an hour later before she saw Ben again and he drew her deliberately to one side.

'Well spotted,' he murmured in an undertone. 'I've sent Mr Gardner for a CT scan but I'd say he's definitely got an extradural haemorrhage.'

She nodded. If a blow to the side of the head fractured the skull it could rupture an artery running over the surface of the dura mater, causing bleeding within or around the brain. Sometimes a patient could momentarily lose consciousness and then apparently recover while all the time a haematoma was forming. If it wasn't treated in time the casualty could lapse into a coma and die.

'What alerted you?' he asked curiously.

'I don't know,' she confessed. 'I suppose the fact that he seemed so confused, and when he said he felt sleepy too...'

'If it is an extradural haemorrhage, he'll need a craniotomy.'

It was a very tricky operation. Holes had to be drilled into the skull to drain the blood clot before the ruptured blood vessel could be clipped, but if Donald Gardner hadn't come in...

'Too many people think a blow to the head is an accepted hazard of playing physical contact sport,' Ben observed, as though he'd read her mind. 'Luckily he came in, and luckily you were concerned about him.'

'Will he be all right?' she said, scanning his face.

'I think so.' He smiled, only for his smile to instantly disappear as a burst of male laughter came from the end of the treatment room.

Izzie turned in the direction of his gaze and groaned inwardly. Steve couldn't have chosen a worse time to enjoy a joke with one of the porters.

'Ben—'

'No, Izzie,' he interrupted firmly.

'You don't even know what I was going to say,' she protested.

'I can guess.'

She bit her lip. 'I didn't realize I was so transparent.'

'Not transparent,' he observed, his voice oddly weary. 'Just too damn loyal.'

'Ben—'

'Who's in 5, Fran?' he asked as the staff nurse emerged from the cubicle.

'A Mrs Anderson. Sixty-two years old. Fell in her garden and she's experiencing quite a lot of pain in her arm.'

Ben nodded. 'Will you assist, Izzie?'

Quickly she glanced across at Fran. As she'd taken Mrs Anderson's particulars she was really her patient but Fran simply smiled back and mouthed across at her, 'Be my guest.'

'Oh, Doctor, I feel such a fool,' Mrs Anderson exclaimed when she saw him. 'All I was doing was hanging out my washing and I tripped.'

Gently he felt along her collar-bone and down her left arm.

'Is the pain very bad?' he murmured, seeing her wince.

'Let's put it this way,' she replied with a crooked smile. 'I've had two children and I'd far rather have a third than go through this.'

'We'll give you something for the pain in a minute,' Ben said sympathetically, 'but first could you grip my hand as tightly as you can?'

Mrs Anderson did as he'd asked. 'My doctor thought I'd just dislocated my shoulder and I'm so hoping he's right,' she said, gazing up at him worriedly. 'My grandchildren are coming to stay, you see, and if it's broken—'

'It's going to make life very difficult for you,' Ben finished for her. 'I'm sorry, but I think your arm *is* broken, Mrs Anderson.'

She sighed. 'Is that why it feels so funny—as though it's hovering about all over the place?'

He nodded. 'Your brain is receiving conflicting signals. You're telling it to do one thing, and it's trying to do something else. I'll give you something to ease the pain and then Sister Clark will take you along to X-Ray to verify my diagnosis.'

'Don't you think it would be better if Tess took her?' Izzie said as soon as she and Ben emerged from the cubicle. 'You know what the queues are like in X-Ray, and if Mrs Anderson's arm *is* broken I could be ages in the plastering department, and if there's an emergency here—'

'We'll cope,' he interrupted. 'I want you to go with her. She looks a bit shaky to me.'

It was true. Mrs Anderson did look decidedly wobbly, but Izzie had the strangest feeling that he was deliberately trying to get rid of her.

'But, Ben—'

'Off you go,' he said firmly. 'The sooner you go, the quicker you'll be back.'

'What bone did that nice young man in X-Ray say I'd broken?' Mrs Anderson asked as Izzie wheeled her back into the treatment room some time later.

'Your humerus.'

'Well, all I can say is that it doesn't feel very funny to me,' Mrs Anderson declared, staring down at her freshly plastered arm wryly.

Izzie chuckled. 'I'll bet it doesn't. Your humerus is the big bone that runs from your shoulder down to your elbow, but luckily you've got what we call a simple fracture so it shouldn't take too long to heal.'

'I was right, then,' Ben said as he came towards them. 'Your arm is broken?'

Mrs Anderson sighed. 'It wouldn't be so bad if I could tell people I'd done it sky-diving or bungee-jumping, but hanging out washing?'

'You'd be surprised at how many accidents happen in and around the home,' Ben observed. 'Considerably more, in fact, than occur when people are taking part in dangerous sports. I've got some pills for you,' he continued, extracting two bottles from his pocket. 'Take one of the dihydrocodeine every four to six hours if the pain gets too bad, but don't drink any alcohol with them or you'll feel drowsy. The diclofenac is to reduce the swelling in your arm—take one of those three times a day with food.'

Mrs Anderson took the pills from him with a distinctly shaky hand and Ben crouched down in front of her.

'Would you like me to arrange for you to stay?'

'I'd far rather go home, Doctor,' she said firmly. 'My husband will take care of me.'

'You're sure?' Ben pressed. 'It would only be for a couple of days, and I understand the food in our wards is almost edible.'

Mrs Anderson managed a small smile. 'Thanks all the same, Doctor, but I'd rather go home.'

Ben didn't look happy but he nodded. 'We'll make an appointment for you to see our orthopaedic surgeon but come back to us immediately if you develop any pins and needles in your fingers or if they suddenly look very white or blue.'

'Nice lady,' Izzie murmured as one of the porters wheeled Mrs Anderson away.

'She is,' Ben agreed. 'Izzie, there's something I'd better tell you—'

'Sorry to interrupt,' Tess said with an apologetic nod at Ben as she popped up beside them, 'but Staff said to tell you that we seem to be running short of steri-strips and disposable syringes.'

'No problem,' Izzie replied. 'I'll get some from our dispensary.'

But it didn't take her long to discover that their supplies of both items were running critically low, and a deep sigh came from her. As usual that meant that her requisition form was stuck in somebody's in-tray, and as usual it also meant she'd be stuck on the phone for half an hour, trying to sort it out.

'I've found some, Tess,' she declared as she heard the door to the dispensary bang open, 'but we're going to have to go carefully—'

'Thanks, Izzie—thanks for nothing!'

She wheeled round, startled, to find herself staring into Steve's furious face, and her heart sank.

'You just couldn't wait, could you?' he continued tightly.

'You just couldn't wait to go running to Farrell to tell him about Donald Gardner!'

'I didn't go running to him,' she protested. 'I tried to talk to you but—'

'So now it's all my fault, is it?' he flared. 'Izzie, can you imagine what it felt like to be told by that pompous, over-bearing prat that it was clearly time I shaped up my ideas if a nurse was a better diagnostician than I was?'

Hot colour washed up her neck. 'Steve, I'm sorry, but I was worried—'

'It's going to look bloody marvellous on my record, isn't it?' he continued as though she hadn't spoken. 'I diagnose a hangover, and what the bloke's really got is an extradural haemorrhage!'

'Ben won't put it on your record—I'm sure he won't. I'll speak to him—'

'Oh, I think you've done more than enough talking already, don't you, babe?' he said angrily. 'In fact, I think it's about time *you* shaped up your ideas and decided whose side you're on!'

'I told you before that it wasn't a question of taking sides,' she retorted. 'And don't call me babe.'

He stared at her in surprise. 'What?'

'You heard me. Don't call me that. It makes me sound like some sort of airhead.'

'I don't know what's got into you recently, sweetie—'

'And don't call me that either,' she said with exaspera-tion. 'I'm not a babe or a sweetie. I'm a grown woman so stop patronising me.'

His blue eyes narrowed. 'You never complained before when I called you that.'

It was true—she hadn't. And she didn't know why it bothered her now, but it did.

'It's Farrell, isn't it?' he said angrily. 'He's the one who's been putting these stupid ideas into your head.'

She swore under her breath as she picked up the syringes

and steri-strips. 'No one's been putting anything into my head. I'm not an idiot, Steve—I can figure things out for myself. Now, let me past before I really lose my temper.'

But he didn't move. Instead his jaw set. 'You're sleeping with him, aren't you?'

'I'm *what*?' she gasped.

'You heard me,' he snapped. 'You're sleeping with him, though God knows how he can still get it up at his age.'

As soon as her hand made its stinging contact with his cheek she was appalled. 'Oh, Steve, I'm sorry,' she whispered. 'I shouldn't—'

'No, no, you shouldn't,' he interrupted, his face chalk-white save for the imprint of her fingers, 'but at least we both know where we stand. It's over, Izzie—what we had is over.'

Her heart contracted inside her. 'Steve, wait. Can't we at least talk about this?'

'What's there to talk about?'

How could he say that? she wondered. How could he simply dismiss all that they'd been to one another so easily? A wave of furious anger welled within her.

'OK, fine!' she cried. 'If that's what you want, fine. In fact, if I never set eyes on you again it will suit me just fine!'

He didn't even argue with her. He just banged out of the door and she bit down hard on her lip as her eyes filled.

What had she done? Yes, he'd made her angry, but to hit him and then say that she didn't care if she never saw him again?

Go after him, Izzie, her mind urged, but as she half started towards the door it was opened again, not by Steve returning to apologise but by Ben.

'Any luck with the steri-strips?' he asked as she turned her back on him quickly, knowing that she couldn't face him right now.

Wordlessly she pushed the boxes along the worktop to

him, praying that he'd simply take them and go—but he
didn't. Instead, she heard him come forward a step.

'Izzie—are you OK?'

She tried to say yes. She tried to say she was perfectly
fine but all that came out was a strangled sob, and the next
thing she knew she was being propelled out of the dispensary and along the corridor in a tight grip.

'W-where are we going?' she hiccuped. 'The steri-
strips—Fran needs them—'

'She can improvise.'

'But—'

'But nothing,' he interrupted. He pushed her through the
door of his office, sat her firmly down on a seat and then
drew up another one for himself in front of her. 'OK,
what's happened?'

Her unshed tears were much too near the surface for
comfort and she had to swallow hard before she could say
anything. 'Nothing—nothing's happened. I'm…I'm just a
bit tired, that's all.'

He shook his head. 'OK, let's try that one again, and
maybe this time you can come up with something a whole
lot more convincing.'

She looked up at him and then away again. 'It's…it's
personal.'

'We're friends, remember?'

Mutely she shook her head.

'Does that mean we're not friends any more, or that
you're not going to tell me?'

It was the concern in his voice that undid her, and before
she could stop them tears began spilling down her cheeks,
hot salty, gulping tears that had her searching frantically
for a handkerchief until a large white one was pressed
firmly into her hands.

'It's Steve, isn't it?' Ben said, his voice suddenly hard
as he leaned forward and took her hands in his. 'I told him
to shape up his ideas and he took it out on you, didn't he?'

'No—no, you're wrong,' she protested, trying desperately to both stem the flow of her tears and pull her hands free from his—without success.

'Tell me what happened, Izzie.'

'It isn't important,' she murmured wretchedly.

'Tell me,' he insisted.

She gazed down at his hands. They were strong hands, fine hands, and her own looked both lost and yet oddly safe clasped between them.

'We…we had a row about…about Donald Gardner,' she gulped. 'He said a lot of things… I said a lot of things…and then…then he told me it was all over between us.'

'He didn't mean it.'

'He did,' she said brokenly, 'and it's all my fault. I should have remembered how much stress he's been under lately. He takes his exams this weekend, you see, and he's worried in case he doesn't pass…and…and…'

Her voice trailed away into silence as a small voice deep inside her suddenly asked why she was finding it necessary to make all these excuses for Steve. You didn't make excuses for someone you loved…did you?

Ben clearly thought the same because a flash of furious anger appeared on his face. 'You're much too damn nice for your own good—you know that, don't you?'

She managed a small hiccuping laugh. 'Maybe, but at twenty-six it's probably a bit late for me to change.'

'Oh, hinny, he'll come back to you,' he said gently. 'Any man who had half a brain would come back to you.'

No, he wouldn't, she thought, ducking her head to try to hide the burning wash of colour that swept over her cheeks as she remembered Steve's accusation.

For a moment Ben said nothing, then he tilted her chin with one finger and searched her face keenly. 'There's something else, isn't there? This row wasn't solely about Donald Gardner, was it?'

'Of course it was,' she muttered, unable to meet his eyes.

'Tell me, Izzie.'

She stared down at his hands again, seeing the fine tendons running down to his fingers, the faint indentation where his wedding ring must once have been. Abstractedly she wondered why he'd taken it off, why he hadn't kept it on in memory of the woman he so clearly still loved.

'He thinks…' Her voice trembled with embarrassment. 'He thinks…you and I… He thinks…'

She heard his sharp intake of breath. She also heard something that sounded very much like a muttered oath before he cleared his throat. 'I'll talk to him.'

Her head shot up. *'What?'*

'I'll tell him he's behaving like a fool. That you and I…' He shrugged ruefully. 'Well, there is no you and I, is there?'

To her dismay her eyes blurred again. 'You'd do that for me?'

He nodded.

'Why?' she couldn't help but ask.

'Because…' His eyes caught hers, and the warmth and gentleness in them was like balm to her aching heart. 'Because I want you to be happy.'

Tears welled in her eyes again and she extricated her hands from his and blew her nose vigorously. 'You know something, Ben Farrell? You're a very kind man.'

An odd smile appeared on his lips—a smile that almost looked as though he were laughing at himself and not very kindly. 'Every woman's big brother, that's me, Izzie.'

She gazed back at him uncertainly and because she didn't know what else to do she reached out and laid her hand against his cheek.

'Ben…'

Her voice trailed away into silence. There was bitterness in his dark grey eyes but for a split second she almost thought she saw something else—something that caused her breath to lodge tight in her throat and her heart to falter.

She thought she saw desire there, desire and a need that was so intense it was almost frightening. Unconsciously her eyes widened in shock and he got to his feet fast.

'I'll talk to him now.'

'No! I mean, he'll still be angry,' she added quickly as he looked at her in surprise. 'Talking won't help—not right now.'

'You're sure?' he said slowly.

She nodded. 'Go back to the department. I'll be along in a minute.'

He made for the door then hesitated. 'Are you going to be all right on your own?'

She managed to smile. 'I'll be fine. I just need a little time to…to…'

He smiled back at her understandingly, but when he'd gone she sat staring at the empty seat in front of her for a long time.

If she'd let Ben speak to Steve he probably could have made everything all right again. She and Steve could have patched things up and they could have gone on as before, but suddenly she'd realised she didn't want to go on as before. Suddenly she'd realised as she'd gazed into Ben's eyes and seen the pain and heartache there that somehow, some way, she'd fallen in love with him.

CHAPTER SEVEN

IZZIE stared across the hospital canteen. Steve was flirting quite outrageously with one of the nurses from Men's Surgical. Just six weeks ago she'd have been devastated, and yet now…

When had she fallen out of love with him? Even more depressingly, had she ever been in love with him at all, or had she just been flattered that someone so handsome could have been interested in someone like her?

But if that was true, what did that make her? Weak and pathetic was the unpalatable answer to that. Ben had said she was weak. Actually, he'd said she was much too nice for her own good but it amounted to the same thing.

A deep sigh broke from her as she pushed aside her unfinished meal and walked out of the canteen without a backward glance. Time and time again over the last week she'd relived that moment in Ben's office. Had she really seen desire in his eyes, or had it simply been a case of wishful thinking? She didn't want it to be but, increasingly, she was coming to the depressing conclusion that it was.

'He's not worth it, Izzie.'

Fran was regarding her, her plump face angry, and Izzie sighed. 'Isn't he?'

'You bet he's not. I can't believe the way he's been behaving—flirting with every eligible woman in the place—'

'You're talking about Steve?' Izzie said with relief.

'Of course I am. Who did—?'

'Fran, what does hinny mean?' Izzie interrupted quickly.

'Hinny?' the staff nurse repeated in surprise, and then

114

her eyes sparkled. 'Hey, it wouldn't happen to be Mr Farrell who called you that, would it?'

'No, of course not,' Izzie answered, fighting down her mounting colour with difficulty.

'But it's a Northumberland expression, and Mr Farrell's the only—'

'Just tell me what it means, Fran, OK?' Izzie demanded.

'OK.' She chuckled. 'It's a sort of endearment.'

'Like babe or sweetie, you mean?' Izzie murmured with disappointment.

'No, nothing like that. It's more…it's kind of like darling.'

Unconsciously Izzie's face softened. 'Is it?'

'It *was* Mr Farrell, wasn't it?' Fran exclaimed with delight. 'Oh, Izzie—'

'Look, there's no need to make a song and dance about it,' she hissed, all too aware that Tess was watching them curiously from across the room. 'It was only a one-off thing—it didn't mean anything.'

'No?' Fran said, looking for all the world like the cat who'd got the cream.

'No,' Izzie repeated firmly.

'But—'

'Did anything interesting come in while I was on my lunch break?' Izzie continued hurriedly, determinedly changing the subject.

For a second Fran's eyes danced then she shook her head. 'It's been pretty quiet all morning, which probably means we're in for one hell of an afternoon.'

She was right. By four o'clock they scarcely had time to breathe, far less think, but the news of one patient immediately brought Izzie to a halt.

'Joey Simpson?' she said with a sinking heart as April handed her the details. 'Six years old—parents called Scott and Laura?'

'That's the one. According to the child, he fell in the garden and hurt his chest, but he's in a pretty poor way.'

'Who brought him in—his mother or his father?'

'Neither. It was Mavis.'

'Mavis?' Izzie exclaimed in surprise. 'You mean our Mavis?'

'The very same,' April nodded. 'Apparently she's a neighbour and was worried about him.'

It was fortunate somebody had been worried about Joey, Izzie thought after she'd eased off his T-shirt. The child's thin chest was covered in a mass of livid bruises, and it was quite obvious that no fall could have caused such injuries.

'It looks like flail chest to me,' Mavis observed as she sat beside the trolley, her hand still wrapped protectively round Joey's. 'Multiple rib fractures.'

'What on earth makes you say that?' Izzie said in amazement.

A smile creased the old lady's face. 'I used to be a nurse, dear.'

'Is that why—?'

'I come here so often?' Mavis finished for her, her faded brown eyes twinkling as Izzie came to an embarrassed halt. 'I've no husband, no family, and, coming here, it's like coming home, you see.'

Izzie did see, and she couldn't remember ever hearing anything quite so sad.

'His parents are doing it to him, aren't they?' Mavis continued as Izzie gently eased Joey onto his side to relieve his laboured breathing. 'Hitting him, I mean?'

'Do you know where they are?' Izzie asked, all too aware she must put an end to this conversation.

'She's at one of her committee meetings, and he's at work. I did try to contact them, but...' Mavis's small face grew angry. 'I'm afraid I was more interested in the boy.

Will it be that big doctor who'll see him—the one with the vile temper and the kind heart?'

Izzie chuckled. 'If you mean Mr Farrell, yes.'

'I like him,' Mavis said unexpectedly. 'He reminds me of somebody I used to know a long time ago.'

'Does he?' Izzie said with interest.

A faint wash of colour crept across Mavis's lined cheeks. 'Like I said, dear,' she declared briskly, 'it was a long time ago. And now I'd better let you get on with your work,' she continued, getting to her feet and opening the cubicle curtains. 'I'll be in Reception if you need me.'

As soon as the curtains were safely closed Izzie took Joey's small hand in hers.

'How did this happen to you, sweetheart?' she asked softly.

He gazed up at her, his grey eyes blank. 'I fell.'

'I don't think so,' she murmured, gently smoothing back his short blond hair. 'I think somebody hit you.'

Fear and indecision appeared in the grey eyes for a second then Joey looked away. 'I fell,' he repeated.

She sighed. She'd get no more out of him at present. Quickly she popped her head round the cubicle and beckoned to Tess.

'But Mr Farrell said he wasn't to be disturbed unless it was really urgent,' Tess declared when Izzie told her to find Ben. 'He's on the phone, giving Supplies merry hell about that order they still haven't fulfilled yet.'

'Get him, Tess.'

'But—'

'Get him, Tess,' Izzie repeated in a tone that brooked no opposition, and as the student nurse went to do as she'd asked she pulled the curtains shut again and stared down at Joey.

Ben had been right. Somebody was abusing the little boy but if it was either one or both of his parents, why hadn't he told someone?

Mentally she flicked through all the books she'd read on child abuse. Fear could stop a child from talking—fear of reprisal, fear of being hurt even more badly—but love could be a factor, too. Many children so desperately wanted their parents to love them that they'd put up with any amount of pain rather than be separated from them.

Through the curtains she could hear Ben talking to Tess, and went out to meet him.

'Trouble?' he asked as soon as he saw her.

'You said you wanted to see Joey Simpson if he ever came back in again.'

He scanned her face. 'It's bad this time, isn't it?'

She nodded. 'It's bad.'

'Are his parents here?' he asked grimly.

She shook her head. 'Mavis brought him in.'

'Our Mavis?' he exclaimed.

'The same. She's trying to contact Scott and Laura at the moment.'

Without a word he motioned to Tess and the two of them disappeared through the curtains, leaving Izzie gazing unhappily after them. That Ben blamed her for Joey's condition was clear, and the awful thing was that he was right. If she'd allowed him to call in the social workers the last time this would never have happened, but it was too late now for 'if onlys'.

Please let Joey be all right, she prayed as she paced the treatment room. Please let Mavis's speedy action result in the little boy's full recovery.

The sound of raised voices from Reception caught her attention and her face hardened. Mrs Simpson had clearly arrived and was demanding to see her son. Well, she had a few sharp words to say to her, too, she thought as she strode down into Reception.

'Oh, Nurse,' Mrs Simpson said with obvious relief as soon as she saw her. 'This reception person says I've got to wait—'

'That's right,' Izzie interrupted. 'If you'd like to come with me, we have a special area through here for relatives—'

'But I don't want to wait,' Laura Simpson broke in angrily. 'I want to see my son. I understand he's been hurt.'

Determinedly Izzie steered her into one of their waiting rooms and closed the door. 'I think he's been hurt for quite a long time, don't you?'

Laura Simpson bristled. 'I'm sure I don't know what you mean.'

'I think you do,' Izzie replied evenly. 'How long has Joey been having trouble with his breathing?'

'His breathing?' Laura repeated. 'There's nothing wrong with his breathing. He fell in the garden a couple of days ago, but you know what he's like, Nurse. He's always falling.'

It took all of Izzie's self-control not to lose her temper, and she sighed with relief when Ben appeared at the door of the waiting room.

'How is he?' Mrs Simpson asked, going to him quickly. 'Can I see him?'

'All in good time,' Ben replied, his voice cold. 'What I want to know is how your son came to suffer such injuries.'

'I already told the nurse. He fell.'

'Mrs Simpson, the last time I saw injuries like these was on the body of a road traffic accident victim,' Ben retorted. 'Your child has flail chest—multiple rib fractures—and, judging by the colour of his bruises, it didn't happen this morning. Didn't you notice that every time he breathed in his chest wall moved in too?'

'I'm not a doctor,' she replied defensively. 'All I know is that he fell.'

Ben's eyes hardened. 'Your son says you and your husband hit him.'

'All children have to be chastised sometimes,' she protested. 'We love our son—'

'But not enough to bring him into hospital when he's clearly very ill indeed,' Ben countered. 'Mrs Simpson, Joey is on a ventilator in Intensive Care, and I think both the police and the social workers will want to discuss with you why he needs to be there.'

Mrs Simpson whitened. 'The police? But the neighbours, my friends…' Hot colour replaced the white in her cheeks. 'What's Joey been saying to you? The boy's a dreadful liar—'

Ben didn't even wait for her to finish. He just turned on his heel in disgust and strode out of the waiting room. Izzie followed him.

'Is he…? Will Joey be all right, do you think?' she asked anxiously.

'I think so—I hope so. The fractures have led to an infection, but neither of his lungs has collapsed so far.'

She gazed up at him unhappily. 'Ben, I'm sorry. If I'd listened to you—if I hadn't been so arrogant, so sure that I was right—'

'We all make mistakes.'

It was true—they did—but the expression in his grey eyes was so distant, so remote, that her heart twisted inside her.

Why had she fallen in love with this man? He wasn't handsome. He had no gift for flowery speeches and compliments, yet she knew without a shadow of a doubt that she'd fallen in love with him.

If only she could talk to him, ask him… Ask him what? Whether he felt the same as she did? Determinedly she shook her head. She could never ask him that, never, and yet she so wanted to know what he was thinking, what he was feeling.

'Ben—'

She didn't get a chance to say any more. The door to the treatment room banged open and Tess yelled down the corridor, 'Priority 1!'

A priority 1 was a possible life-threatening emergency, and as one Izzie and Ben raced towards her.

'What is it—what's happened?' he demanded.

'Alex Wilson—seven years old—knocked off his bicycle in the square and brought in with minor abrasions,' the student nurse replied, visibly shaken. 'I was cleaning his cuts when he suddenly collapsed.'

'Where is he?'

'In the resuscitation room with Dr Melville and Staff Nurse Walton.'

Ben nodded, but as he turned on his heel a white-faced, distraught woman caught him convulsively by the arm.

'Oh, Doctor, please… He's my son…my only child. Please…please don't let him die. Please help him!'

'I'll do my best, I promise,' Ben replied, motioning to Tess who quickly wrapped a protective arm around the woman and led her away. 'Izzie,' he continued, turning to her, 'you'd better come with me.'

By the time they'd reached the resuscitation room Steve had already inserted a tube into the child's windpipe to assist his breathing and Fran had linked him to a heart monitor.

'OK, what have we got?' Ben asked, rolling up his sleeves.

'Damned if I know,' Steve replied. 'He was right as rain one minute and then suddenly he just keeled over.'

'You found nothing unusual when you examined him?' Ben demanded, taking his stethoscope out of his pocket.

'I thought I heard an odd murmur when I was sounding him—'

'Odd?' Ben interrupted. 'What kind of odd?'

'A sort of whooshing sound.'

'Could be an aortic aneurysm.' Ben frowned. 'Steve, set up a IV line. Izzie, watch the oxygen intake— Oh, for God's sake, give that to me,' he continued with a flash of anger as the cannula slipped out of Steve's fingers. 'By the time you get it inserted the child could be dead!'

Scarlet colour swept over Steve's cheeks and deliberately Izzie avoided his eyes. It didn't surprise her that he was all fingers and thumbs. Ben had been riding him pretty hard ever since he'd misdiagnosed Donald Gardner's extradural haemorrhage.

'Cardiac arrest!' Fran yelled suddenly.

'Lignocaine,' Ben demanded.

Quickly Izzie handed him the syringe.

'Pulse and BP reading?' he demanded after he'd inserted it into Alex Wilson's arm.

'No pulse, no BP,' Fran replied.

'Damn, *damn*! ECG reading, Steve?'

'None.'

'OK, hands off, everyone,' Ben ordered as he picked up the metal plates by the side of the trolley and placed them on each side of the boy's small chest. 'Any change?' he demanded as the child's body convulsed with the force of the electrical current.

'None,' Steve replied, his voice taut.

'Beryllium, Izzie.'

Swiftly she administered the drug. Again Ben attempted to shock the child's heart into life and again, until at last he threw the paddles onto the trolley with a muttered oath and switched off the defibrillator. 'OK, that's enough.'

A depressed silence fell over the resuscitation room. It was always like this when they lost a patient—the feeling of inadequacy, of failure—and it was Ben who broke the silence.

'Look, we've got other patients waiting so could we please get back to work?' he snapped.

Steve and Fran disappeared fast but Izzie stayed where she was.

'You did your best,' she murmured.

'Yeah, right,' he replied, his mouth twisting. 'I expect Mrs Wilson will be thrilled to bits to hear that.'

She winced but before she could say anything he wearily ran his hands through his black hair. 'I'm sorry. That was totally uncalled-for.'

'I'm sorry, too,' she said awkwardly, taking a step towards him. 'Sorry about Alex, sorry about Joey and sorry that I've added to your troubles as well.'

'You?' he exclaimed. 'You haven't done anything.'

'But I have,' she insisted. 'I involved you in my private life and that wasn't right or fair. Steve and I—'

He reached out and clasped one of her hands in his. 'Izzie, let me talk to him. I can make it right for you, I know I can.'

Tell him it isn't Steve you want but him, a little voice urged at the back of her mind, but she couldn't. Instead she drew a steadying breath.

'Ben, do you think Steve and I are right for one another?'

For a moment he was silent and desperately she willed him to say they weren't right for one another, that he loved her more than Steve ever could, but he didn't. He simply cleared his throat and said, 'That's not for me to say.'

'Perhaps it isn't,' she pressed, her eyes fixed on him, 'but I'd still value your opinion.'

For a moment his fingers tightened around hers and then he released her hand. 'I want…' He paused, and when he spoke his voice was oddly rough. 'I want whatever you want, Izzie. And now I must go,' he continued abruptly. 'Mrs Wilson will be waiting for me.'

A hard lump formed in her throat as she watched him walk away. Part of her longed to go after him and part of her wanted to burst into tears, but she knew she could do neither. Mrs Wilson would want to see her son and she couldn't let her see him like this—connected to a battery of machines.

Wearily she disconnected the heart and oxygen ma-

chines, and had just finished covering the child with a clean
sheet when Mrs Wilson arrived.

'Would you like me to stay with you?' Izzie asked
gently, as the woman slowly approached the trolley.

'No,' she whispered. 'I'd rather…I'd prefer to be alone,
if you don't mind.'

Izzie's heart went out to her, but relatives had to deal
with their grief in their own way and quietly she slipped
out of the room, only to walk straight into Sister Faith
Norman.

'It's not time for your shift already, is it, Faith?' she said
in surprise.

'Already?' she chuckled. 'I came on duty nearly an hour
ago, Izzie.'

Which meant that Ben had gone home. Gone home,
without even saying goodnight.

'Look, I hate to do this to you when you've clearly had
a bad day,' Faith continued as she dived into her pocket,
'but Mr Farrell seems to have left his pager behind and I
was wondering whether you could drop it off at his cottage
on your way home.'

'But that's not—'

'Not what?' Faith asked curiously as Izzie stared down
at the pager in her hand.

It wasn't Ben's—it was Steve's—and yet Izzie found
herself reaching for it.

'Of course I'll take it to him,' she said. 'No problem.'

She wasn't nearly as self-assured, however, by the time she
drew her car to a halt outside Keeper's Cottage some time
later.

You're an idiot, Izzie Clark, she decided as she gazed
out at the low, grey stone building. One look at the pager
will tell Ben it isn't his, and one look at your face will tell
him you know it isn't his.

Oh, stop being such a wimp, she told herself. So what if

he realises you're simply using the pager as an excuse to call by? You're friends, aren't you? And friends visit one another all the time.

Yes, but friends don't normally spend nearly half an hour in the hospital toilets, carefully applying make-up before dropping in on someone, her mind pointed out as she walked down the overgrown path and pressed the doorbell. Friends don't feel half sick, half excited, if all they're doing is paying a casual call.

Oh, why don't you just mind your own damn business? she told the annoying little voice. He might not even be home. He might be out or... Hot colour suddenly flooded her cheeks. What if he was home, but not alone? What if Joanna was with him, and they were...

Frantically she turned on her heel but she was too late. Ben was standing on the doorstep and his expression was anything but welcoming.

'Izzie,' he said slowly. 'What an unexpected surprise.'

And not a very pleasant one, she thought with a sinking heart as she stared into a pair of grey eyes that held neither warmth nor pleasure.

'You...you left your pager behind at the hospital,' she began hurriedly. 'And I...Sister Norman and I...were worried in case you were concerned about it.'

He gazed down at the pager and then at her. 'It isn't mine.'

'Isn't it?' she said, all too aware that her voice sounded unnaturally high.

He shook his head. 'It's Steve's, so if there's nothing else....?'

Oh, God, he was actually going to shut the door on her.

'I-I'm sorry to have disturbed you,' she stammered. 'I-I should have realised. I-I should have known. I-I'm sorry.'

And with that she bolted down the path only to find when she reached her car that he had followed her.

'That wasn't very gracious of me, was it?' he said, his

cheeks almost as flushed as hers. 'Look, I'm just about to have dinner. Would you like to join me?'

Did he mean it, or was he simply being polite? She decided on the latter and shook her head. 'You can't possibly have enough food—'

'Izzie, I wouldn't have invited you if I hadn't wanted you to accept,' he interrupted with a brusqueness that made her blink. 'Dinner will be ready in ten minutes.'

He didn't even wait for her reply. He just whirled on his heel and strode back down the path into the house, clearly expecting her to follow—and after a moment's hesitation she did.

'Is there anything I can do to help?' she asked as he came to a halt in the middle of the hall. 'Peel some potatoes, lay the table?'

He shook his head. 'Please, make yourself at home.'

How? she wondered as he walked away. How could she make herself at home when he clearly didn't want her here, when it was quite obvious that she should never have come?

Unhappily she wandered into the sitting room. He hadn't changed anything since Miss Benson's day, apart from adding some modern paintings. The dark oak beams, the polished wooden floor, the lovely old oak furniture—they were all still the same. But where once she'd felt totally at ease and comfortable, she now felt completely alien.

'What do you think of my home?' Ben asked, appearing without warning behind her.

'It's lovely,' she replied.

His eyebrows lifted. 'Do I sense a ''but'' in there?'

'Not a ''but'' exactly.' She smiled. 'It's just that if it were mine, I'd—'

'You'd fill it with ornaments and tapestry cushions to make it more homey.'

It was so exactly what she'd been thinking that she flushed. 'How did you guess?'

'You told me once that you were a romantic, remember?'

He didn't make it sound like a compliment and the colour on her cheeks deepened. Why, oh, why had she come? She should never have come, and as the silence between them lengthened she glanced desperately round the room, trying to think of something—anything—to say.

'Unusual paintings,' she said at last.

'Unusual?' he repeated.

Damn depressing would have been closer to the mark, but not for the world would she have said so. The huge landscape, the smaller seascape and the painting of the red-headed girl in a field of poppies gave her the shivers. They were so dark and wild, as though the person who had painted them had been desperately unhappy.

'Different, I mean,' she said quickly. 'They're…they're different.'

'You don't like them?'

She gave up. 'Let's just say I wouldn't want them on my walls.'

'I painted them.'

There was no point in apologising. She couldn't take back what she'd said and, as she followed him through to the dining room, she could only pray that the evening wouldn't deteriorate still further.

But it did.

The food was lovely. The trout was clearly freshly caught. The salad and small potatoes that accompanied it were crisp and sweet, but Izzie knew that she could have been eating stale bread for all the difference it would have made.

He doesn't love you, her heart kept saying as they ate their meal in virtual silence. He doesn't even seem to *like* you very much tonight, and yet she was all too aware of him.

Make some excuses to leave, her heart begged every time his fingers curled round his wine glass and she found her-

self imagining those fingers curled round her body. Tell
him you have another appointment, her mind urged as she
felt her breath catch every time he reached for something
and his white shirt tightened tantalisingly across the muscles of his broad chest.

'Ben—'

'Izzie—'

They'd spoken in unison, and it was she who said, 'You
first.'

For a moment he said nothing and she waited, aware that
her palms felt slightly damp and that her heart was beating
unnaturally fast.

'Izzie, it's about Steve.'

Her throat tightened. 'I don't want to talk about Steve.'

'Izzie, I admire your independence but, please, won't you
let me help you?'

There's only one way you can do that, she thought miserably, and you clearly won't, not ever. Blindly she reached
for her knife and fork only to notice too late that he had
moved the bottle of wine closer to her. Too late she felt
her elbow catch it, and a cry of horror sprang from her lips
as the bottle went crashing to the floor, sending wine and
broken glass everywhere.

'Oh, God, I'm sorry,' she cried, leaping to her feet immediately. 'The wine, your floor—your beautiful floor!'

'It doesn't matter.'

'It does. I'll get a cloth—'

'Izzie, it really doesn't matter,' he insisted, catching her
arm to restrain her. 'I don't give a damn about the stupid
bottle or the floor.'

'But I do,' she protested. 'I—I come here uninvited, in-
sult your pictures, eat your dinner, and then to cap it all I
ruin your floor. I'm hopeless... I can't do anything right.'

'Oh, Izzie, I'm the one who should be apologising,' he
exclaimed. 'I've been so rude to you tonight, and then to
be so tactless, mentioning Steve...'

How could he be so blind? she wondered as she stared up at him. Couldn't he see she was in love with him, or did he simply feel so little for her that it had never even occurred to him?

Tears welled in her eyes at the thought and she scrabbled in her pocket for a handkerchief. God, but he must think she was so pathetic—bursting into tears all the time—but he didn't seem to find her pathetic. In fact, he immediately drew her firmly into his arms.

'Ah, hinny, don't,' he said, his voice cracking. 'Please… I can't bear to see you cry.'

Why did he have to call her that when she knew very well that he didn't mean it? If he'd called her anything else she might have been able to stop her tears, but not that, not that.

'Oh, Izzie, don't,' he murmured into her hair as she sobbed into the broad warmth of his chest. 'I'll get him back for you. I promise I will.'

'You don't understand,' she hiccuped miserably. 'You…you just don't understand.'

'I do—believe me, I do,' he declared, lifting her head gently and then even more gently stroking the tears from her cheeks with his fingers. 'I know exactly what heartbreak is.'

She tried to speak but her tongue felt as though it had cleaved to the roof of her mouth. She wanted to tell him that he was wrong, so wrong, but her entire body seemed to be dissolving under the influence of those feather-light fingers.

Actions speak louder than words, Izzie, a small voice urged at the back of her head, and before she could change her mind she reached up and tentatively brushed his lips with her own. His eyes widened and darkened but she didn't stop. Again she brushed his lips, and again, and at the third time a sob lodged in her throat as his lips came down on hers with a groan that seemed wrenched from somewhere deep inside him.

There was nothing gentle about his kiss this time, nothing tentative. His mouth and tongue were bruising, demanding, as though this was a man who'd held himself in check for too long, and when his fingers cupped the soft roundness of her breasts, sought for and found her hardening nipples, a soft moan of ecstasy broke from her.

He does want you, her drumming heart cried with joy. He does love you, her body sang as she eased herself closer to him and felt his body stirring and hardening against hers. And she wanted him. The pulsing, slippery rush between her thighs told her how much so that when he suddenly thrust her away she gazed at him in bewilderment.

'Ben…?' she faltered, her breathing fast and erratic, 'Ben—'

'I think you'd better go.'

His voice was low but the meaning was clear enough and she stared at him blankly.

'Go?' she echoed.

'Izzie…' He clenched his hands together until the knuckles showed white. 'I think…I think you're a lovely girl, a very special girl, but this is crazy. Steve—'

'Will you stop talking about Steve?' she said crossly. 'I don't want Steve, I'm not in love with Steve. I'm…I'm in love with you.'

There, it was said, and her cheeks flushed crimson as he gazed at her, his eyes strained.

'Izzie…' He paused and cleared his throat. 'Izzie, I'm immensely flattered that someone like you could even for one minute believe herself to be in love with me, but you're not.'

'I am,' she cried in frustration. 'Ben, I think I've been falling in love with you for weeks.'

Something blazed in his eyes for a second—hope or horror—and then it was gone.

'Even if that were true,' he said with an effort, 'I'm all wrong for you. I'm too old—too dull, too boring.'

'You're not dull and boring,' she protested. 'And you're certainly not old.'

'Izzie, I was practising medicine when you were still playing with dolls.'

'I've never played with dolls in my life,' she exclaimed. 'Bows and arrows—yes—but never dolls.'

A slight smile curved his lips but disappeared just as quickly. 'It wouldn't work, Izzie. When Caroline died...'

He came to a halt and she wanted to shout at him, to scream at him that his wife was dead, that she wouldn't ever come back, but she didn't.

'You're still in love with her, aren't you?' she said instead, her voice quivering.

He didn't answer, and she reached for him but he backed away.

'Ben—'

'Go home, Izzie,' he said wearily. 'Go home before I do something we'll both regret for the rest of our lives.'

'But I wouldn't regret it,' she whispered, conscious that her cheeks were burning. 'I...I want you, and I know...I could tell that you...you want me.'

For a second she thought he might take her back into his arms again and then to her horror he threw back his head and laughed mockingly. 'Of course I want you! I'm a man, for God's sake, not a monk, and when an attractive young woman throws herself at me what the hell would you expect me to do?'

She flinched and, seeing it, his lip curled. 'Oh, for God's sake, go home, Izzie. This is no place for a country hick and, believe me, you're way out of your depth here.'

Her eyes were so full of tears she could barely see his face. 'Ben, please—'

'What does it take to get through to you?' he flared. 'I don't want you here so why don't you just get out?'

And with a strangled sob she did.

She didn't know that he watched her until her car was no more than a faint pinprick on the horizon. She didn't know that he then walked slowly back into the house and poured himself a large whiskey. And she didn't know that he stood staring at the painting of the red-headed girl in a field of poppies for a very long time before he suddenly hurled his glass at it with a cry of despair.

CHAPTER EIGHT

'Izzie, we have to talk.'

Ben's voice was soft but insistent, and her heart sank. If only she hadn't stopped to talk to Faith Norman. If she hadn't stopped she'd have been halfway home by now, instead of walking straight into the one person she'd been desperately trying to avoid all morning.

'Can't it wait, Ben?' she said quickly. 'This is my half-day—'

'It's mine too, and, no, it can't,' he declared, preventing her escape by the simple expedient of putting his hands against the wall on either side of her. 'Izzie, we have to talk about what happened last night at my cottage.'

She didn't want to talk about it. Even thinking about what she'd said, and how he'd reacted, was enough to make her cringe with embarrassment.

'Please,' she whispered, her eyes darting down the corridor in the vain hope that somebody—anybody—would appear and put an end to a conversation she'd prefer not to have. 'Please, you don't have to say anything. I...I understand perfectly.'

'I doubt it,' he murmured. 'Izzie, look at me.'

She didn't want to look at him. She didn't want to meet his eyes and perhaps see pity or even amusement there, but she forced her gaze up and saw neither pity nor amusement in the grey eyes that stared down at her—only a gentle concern that was somehow worse.

'Izzie, we were both very vulnerable last night,' he began slowly. 'You because of Steve, and me...' A tiny muscle quivered for an instant at the corner of his mouth and then

133

his lips tightened. 'But that doesn't excuse what I said to you. I should never—'

The shrill sound of his pager interrupted him and, as he reached into his pocket to answer it, she took to her heels and ran.

It was only postponing the inevitable. Ben would undoubtedly return to the subject again, but right now she didn't care. Right now all she wanted was to go home, shut the door and wish she'd never been born.

'It looks bad, doesn't it, Sister?' one of the porters commented as she crossed the road to her car.

'Catastrophic's closer to the mark,' she murmured, and then flushed as the porter gazed at her curiously. 'Sorry, Bill, I was thinking about something else. What looks bad?'

'The fire in Houndslow's Timber Yard. Lots of casualties, so I hear.'

For a second she just stared at him and then suddenly she was running—running back into the hospital.

'That was a short afternoon off.' Faith Norman grinned when she saw her.

'Glutton for punishment, that's me,' Izzie replied ruefully. 'What's the situation?'

'Six casualties on the way so far—three women, one female passerby and two firemen,' Faith said, and then chuckled as Ben appeared through the doors of the treatment room. 'Couldn't keep away either, Mr Farrell? Must be my magnetic charm.'

'Something like that.' He smiled. 'What have we got in at the moment that can't wait?'

'Acute asthma attack in 3, pneumonia in 5 and a possible ectopic in 2,' Steve replied as he joined them.

Ben nodded. 'Send the asthma and pneumonia cases straight up to the wards and page Mr Brownlie in Gynae for the ectopic. Faith, alert Theatre, Radiography, and the labs to be on standby. Izzie, check the equipment in the resuscitation room and, Tess—'

'When the casualties get here, monitor their ABCs. It's what Sister Clark always says,' she added uncertainly as Ben's eyebrows rose. 'The first priority with any patient is to check their airways, breathing and circulation—their ABCs.'

'She's absolutely right,' he observed. 'And she's clearly an excellent teacher.'

Please, don't praise me, Izzie thought miserably as they all scattered to carry out his instructions. I don't want your praise. In fact, I'd far rather you totally ignored me from now on, and then maybe—just maybe—I might eventually be able to forget that I made a complete and utter fool of myself last night.

And what a fool, she thought with mortification as she swiftly checked the equipment in the resuscitation room. How could she have thrown herself at him the way she had? How could she have told him that she loved him?

And he'd tried so hard to stop her, she remembered. Saying he was too old for her, too boring, when the humiliating truth was that he simply didn't want her. He wanted Joanna. Joanna, who was exactly the same age as she but who wasn't big and ordinary but petite and beautiful.

Stop thinking about it, she told herself as she went back to the treatment room in time to see the doors clatter open and the first of the casualties arrive. You've got enough to think about at present, without dwelling on something you can't change.

'This poor bloke's one of the firemen,' the paramedics declared as she helped them lift the middle-aged man from the stretcher onto the trolley. 'Name of David Renton. BP 90 over 70, cardiac output down thirty per cent.'

For a second Izzie gazed, transfixed, at the fireman's appallingly burned face and body, then her years of training took over. If they didn't increase the blood flow through

David Renton's tissues quickly, he'd develop hypothermia and go into shock.

'I'll renew his haemeccel drip,' Ben said, appearing at her side without warning. 'You start cutting off his uniform.'

She nodded but when she reached for the scissors the fireman tried to push her away.

'See to the men who were working in Houndslow's first, lass,' he whispered hoarsely. 'I'm fine—honestly I am. In fact, apart from my face, I don't feel any pain at all.'

It was the worst possible admission. If David Renton felt no pain from the burns he'd sustained then not only the skin on his chest and legs but also the nerves beneath it must have been totally destroyed.

'I'm sure they're all being well taken care of, Mr Renton,' Izzie said reassuringly as Ben linked him to a heart monitor. 'You just relax.'

'Pulse, Sister?' Ben demanded.

With practically no skin left at all on David Renton's wrist or throat, the only way she could get a pulse was by holding a Doppler probe over the carotid area and reading the ultrasound echo back from the oscilloscope.

'One-thirty and rising, Mr Farrell,' she replied, and saw a frown crease Ben's forehead.

It wasn't good, it wasn't good at all—nor was the dark urine that was collecting in the Foley catheter that Ben had inserted into David Renton's bladder to check for signs of haemoglobin or myoglobin. And when a paroxysm of coughing suddenly gripped the fireman, and black sputum trickled down his chin, Ben's eyes met hers.

It looked very much as though the fireman's stomach or bowel had been blocked because of smoke inhalation, and if he wasn't operated on quickly...

Swiftly Izzie pulled back the cubicle curtains and within seconds the fireman was being wheeled towards the Theatre.

'What are his chances?' she said as Ben peeled off his surgical gloves and threw them into the disposal bin.

'With those burns and a blockage...'

His voice died away and she risked a glance up at him. There were dark smudges under his eyes—smudges which suggested he hadn't slept well last night. She hadn't slept at all. She'd tossed and turned all night, dreading the moment when she'd have to meet him again, talk to him.

As though he'd read her mind, he suddenly cleared his throat and panic welled within her. Oh, dear God, no. Surely he wasn't going to say something about last night— not now when anyone could, and would, hear him?

'Izzie, I need some help over here!' Steve yelled from across the room, and she sped across to him with relief and didn't hear Ben's muttered oath as he watched her.

What the hell was the matter with him? he wondered. She obviously didn't want to remember what had happened last night and it was the best thing—the only thing—they could both do if they wanted to continue working together, but he couldn't forget. No matter how hard he tried, he just couldn't forget the look on her face when he'd told her to get out, that he didn't want her.

And he had wanted her. God help him, he still did, he thought angrily, digging his fists deep into the pockets of his white coat.

'Forget it, Ben,' he murmured, seeing Fran beckoning frantically to him. 'Forget it, because no woman in her right mind would want what you've got to offer.'

'Thank God that's the last of them,' Steve exclaimed wearily as he watched the final few non-urgent victims from the fire at Houndslow's leave A and E. 'I'm absolutely shattered.'

'Snap,' Izzie replied, massaging the ache at the base of her spine in a vain attempt to ease it.

They'd been working flat out for over three hours and it felt like every bone in her body was protesting.

'We all did pretty well, considering,' Steve commented, bending to retrieve a discarded dressing from the floor. 'I was a bit worried about Tess at the beginning, but she coped really well.'

Izzie nodded proudly. The student nurse may occasionally have looked a bit green about the gills, but she'd never once faltered.

'But the main star of the afternoon has got to be you, Izzie,' Steve continued. 'I mean it,' he added as she shook her head and laughed. 'I always knew you were good, but I didn't realise just how good.'

'Hey, you weren't so bad yourself,' she said, laughing a little shakily at the clear admiration in his blue eyes.

And he had been good. In fact, he'd been so professional all afternoon that she wondered if he might have received the results of his exams. Guiltily she remembered that she hadn't even wished him good luck when he'd sat them but, then, they hadn't exactly been talking since that afternoon in the dispensary.

Much the same thought must have occurred to him because he suddenly shifted his shoulders uncomfortably. 'Izzie, there's something I want to say to you. Something I should have said a long time ago. Izzie—Izzie, are you listening to me?'

She wasn't. Out of the corner of her eye she could see Ben strolling down the room. To the casual observer it might look as though he was merely checking the cubicles, but she knew better. He was waiting. Waiting for an opportunity to catch her alone, and she knew only too well what he wanted to talk about.

'Later, Steve, OK?' she murmured, reaching for her handbag. 'I'll talk to you later.'

'But, Izzie—'

She didn't even let him finish. The second she saw Faith

Norman engage Ben in conversation she was out of A and E like a shot.

Home, she told herself as she drove the short distance from the hospital to her flat. Once you get home you'll feel better, but as soon as she opened the door of her flat she knew that she couldn't stay there for the remainder of the afternoon. It was too quiet, too oppressive.

A walk, she decided, showering quickly and changing into a long patterned skirt and short-sleeved blouse. A walk through Kelso would give her something else to think about.

However, walking past the Ednam House, she was simply reminded of the day Ben had taken her there. Crossing Bridge Street and seeing the Queen's Head, that only brought back memories of the meals she'd shared with Steve and how once—oh, it seemed like a lifetime ago now—she'd hoped they might marry if he passed his exams. Now he wasn't a part of her life any more. And the man she wanted… Her eyes blurred slightly. He would never be a part of her life.

She took the path that led down to the river. There, at least, there'd be no memories. Steve hadn't been much of a walker, and Ben… Determinedly she shook her head. She wasn't going to think about Ben. She was simply going to walk and admire the beauty of the scenery, and then hopefully she might be able to sleep tonight.

And the scenery was beautiful, she acknowledged as she walked on, gradually losing all track of time—Floors Castle, shimmering rose pink under the early evening sun, the Tweed, sparkling and dancing as a slight breeze got up, and in the distance the stunning purple of the Eildon Hills.

Don't think about the Eildons, she told herself as she rounded a bend in the river to see a solitary fisherman, casting his line. If you think about the Eildons it will only remind you of Ben. But as the fisherman suddenly glanced

over his shoulder she saw to her horror that she didn't need
reminding of him—not when he was there in the flesh.

For a second she stood transfixed to the spot, totally unable to move, but when he threw down his rod and began
clambering up the bank, panic galvanised her into action.

'Izzie, wait!' he called after her.

Not on your life, she thought, quickening her steps to a
run, but his legs were much longer than hers and he soon
caught up with her.

'Izzie—'

'What?' she demanded, turning on him, her nerves in
shreds. 'What do you want?'

A flush of embarrassed colour appeared in his cheeks, as
though he'd come after her on impulse and now wasn't
altogether certain of what he should say.

'Look, this isn't the most convenient place to talk,' he
said awkwardly. 'Why don't I take you into town—buy you
a coffee?'

'It must be well after six, Ben. All the cafés will be
closed.'

'A drink, then—or how about a meal?'

She gazed up at him wearily. She was tired of running,
tired of trying to avoid him—she just wanted it over with.

'Ben, you don't have to take me for a drink or a meal.'
She sighed. 'I know what you want to talk about and, believe me, there's no need. I behaved like a complete fool
last night and all I can do is apologise and suggest we both
try to forget it.'

He knew he should have felt relieved, but all he could
see was the strain in her deep brown eyes, the nervous way
she kept pleating and unpleating her fingers, and he took a
step forward.

'Izzie, I owe you an explanation.'

'You don't,' she said firmly. 'You don't owe me anything except perhaps a promise that you won't tell Joanna
about what happened last night.'

'Joanna?' he said, puzzled. 'Why should I tell Joanna?'

'Because you and she are dating, aren't you?'

Clear exasperation appeared on his face. 'This hospital and its bloody rumours! Izzie, I've taken her out once, and that was only because the blasted woman twisted my arm, saying she wanted to discuss a possible donation to the hospital.'

Her heart soared only to plummet again just as quickly. So he wasn't interested in Joanna—so what? He still didn't want her.

'Izzie, listen to me—'

'I've got to go,' she interrupted, backing away from him, anxious to be gone. 'I'll see you at work tomorrow.'

'But—'

'Ben, there's no point in dissecting what happened,' she continued, backing away from him still further. 'I made a fool of myself and that's all there is to it.'

'Izzie, will you watch what you're doing?' he said with concern, gazing for some unknown reason at a spot behind her. 'You're getting too near the—'

'I know you're trying to be kind,' she broke in. 'I know you're trying to make me feel better, but—'

'Izzie, watch out! *Izzie!*'

For a second she almost recovered her balance. For a second as her feet slipped out from under her she almost caught hold of his hand as he lunged towards her, but the incline was too steep, her shoes too soft, and with a sharp cry she tumbled straight back into the cold waters of the Tweed.

'Put your feet down!' Ben yelled as she surfaced, gasping and choking for breath. 'It's not that deep—put your feet down!'

He was right. The water came no higher than midway up her thighs, but when she got unsteadily to her feet and pushed her soaking wet hair back from her face tears of humiliation and anger filled her eyes. He was laughing. The rat fink was actually laughing—and at her.

'Oh, Izzie, I'm sorry,' he choked as she ignored his outstretched hand and clambered back onto the bank without a word. 'I know I shouldn't have laughed, but—'

'You just couldn't help it,' she finished for him tightly. 'It's OK. Everyone else laughs at me so why should you be the exception?'

'I didn't say that,' he exclaimed, grasping her by the arm, his face suddenly angry. 'And I sure as hell didn't mean it.'

'No?' she said defiantly, pulling her arm free.

'No! And where the hell do you think you're going?' he demanded as she turned on her heel and began walking away from him with as much dignity as she could manage, with water and reeds dripping from her.

'Home,' she replied.

'Like that?' he protested. 'Izzie, it's three miles back to Kelso—you'll catch pneumonia.'

'So I'll catch pneumonia,' she declared dismissively.

'Look, my car's just over there,' he declared, pointing to the immaculate BMW parked under the trees. 'I'll drive you home.'

'I prefer to walk,' she replied, her accent clipped.

'I didn't ask what you preferred,' he retorted. 'I said I'd drive you home.'

'And I said I'd rather walk,' she snapped back.

'Izzie, if you don't get in that car right now, I swear I'll pick you up and put you in it.'

Her jaw dropped. 'Y-you wouldn't,' she spluttered. 'Y-you couldn't!'

He folded his arms across his chest and drew himself up to his full height. 'Try me.'

Instinctively she took a step back. For a second she'd forgotten just how big he actually was. He could do it and, judging by the set of his jaw, he would.

'Very well,' she replied. She attempted to sound totally indifferent but unfortunately her voice shook. 'You can drive me home.'

And I hope I ruin your expensive upholstery, she added mentally as he retrieved his fishing rod. I hope all this mud and water drips down into your car's electrics and it costs you an absolute fortune to replace them.

She sat in stony silence as he eased the car up the rough track to the main road, but when he turned right at the top, instead of left, she turned to him quickly. 'This isn't the way back to Kelso.'

'I know.'

'So where are we going?'

'Home—to my home.'

'But—'

'It's nearer.'

'But—'

'It's my car, and I'm driving, Izzie.'

For one wild moment she wondered if she could possibly jump out, only to swiftly dismiss the idea. With her current run of bad luck she'd probably end up breaking her neck.

Well, he could take her back to his house, she told herself, but there was no way he could keep her there. As soon as she'd dried herself as best she could, he wouldn't see her for dust.

That, at least, was her plan, but Ben clearly had other ideas. As soon as they reached his house he steered her firmly up the stairs and into the bathroom.

'What you need is to get warmed up as quickly as possible,' he declared, turning on the taps, 'so I suggest you take a long, hot bath. It makes sense, wouldn't you say?' he added as she gazed at him blankly.

It made perfect sense. She'd left a trail of muddy puddles all the way up the stairs, she was chilled to the bone and there was something unspeakably slimy down the front of her blouse. And yet to take off her clothes, to get into his bath…

'The door has a lock on it,' he continued, clearly reading her mind, and she flushed.

'I didn't say… I know perfectly well that you wouldn't ever…'

She floundered to a scarlet-cheeked halt and he shook his head.

'You know, that's the most depressing thing I've ever heard.'

'W-what?' she stammered.

'Forget it.' He sighed. 'Now, have you everything you need? Soap, towels, hair-drier? What about your clothes—do you need help, taking them off?'

She shook her head vigorously. Her clothes might be sticking to her like glue but she'd get them off herself if she had to use her teeth to do it.

'Chuck them outside and I'll put them in the washing machine,' he said as he strode to the door.

'But—'

'Hey, there's no need to look so worried,' he continued, his lips curving slightly. 'I'm sure I can find you something to wear. Failing that, we can always wrap you up in brown paper.'

'I'm not going around looking like a parcel for anyone,' she protested, but it was too late. He'd already gone.

You don't have to take this, she told herself as she stared down at the steaming water. There's a bus stop at the end of the road and it wouldn't take you more than ten minutes to reach it.

But the water in the bath looks so inviting, she thought, so very inviting. Just half an hour, she decided as she began peeling off her sodden clothes. Just half an hour under those warm, inviting waters and then she'd go home.

But it was more than an hour later when she popped her head nervously round the bathroom door to find not the brown paper he'd threatened her with but a tartan shirt and a pair of corduroy trousers that clearly belonged to him, hanging on the doorhandle.

The trousers fitted her like a glove. OK, so the legs were too long and she had to roll them up, but that still didn't alter the fact that they fitted. At least the shirt was way too big. The shoulders were massive and her hands kept disappearing up into the sleeves, but somehow that didn't make up for the trousers.

She grimaced at her reflection, before padding out of the bathroom and along the landing.

She'd never been upstairs in her old schoolteacher's day and she wondered abstractedly what the rooms up here were like. Would they have the same solid oak floors and small latticed windows as the rooms downstairs, or would they have been modernised? Unfortunately she'd never know. All the doors were closed—all, that was, save one.

Don't be nosy, a warning voice whispered in her ear as she came to a halt. One little peep won't do any harm, she argued back, gently easing the door open, only to let out a startled gasp.

The room was obviously Ben's studio. Paintings and drawings were scattered everywhere, but that wasn't what had caused her exclamation. It was the painting propped up on the easel, the painting that was of her.

And yet not really of her, she thought as she took a step forward to examine it. No twentieth-century woman gazed back at her from the canvas, but a girl who looked as though she belonged within the pages of a fairy story. A girl whose hair was wild and corn-coloured. A girl whose dress was long and green and virtually transparent. Hot colour crawled up the back of her neck as she stared at the girl's figure. That wasn't her body. Her waist wasn't so slender, her hips weren't so slim and as for her breasts...

'What do you think of it?' a low voice asked behind her,

and she whirled round guiltily to find herself staring up into
Ben's grey eyes.

'I—I didn't mean to pry—h-honestly, I didn't,' she stammered. 'The door was open and—'

'What do you think?' he repeated. 'Of the painting?'

A fresh wash of colour crept up her neck as she turned
back to it. 'Is that...is that really how you see me?'

'When you told me that story about the queen of the
elves I just knew that was how I wanted to paint you,' he
said. 'You don't like it?' he added, when she said nothing.

'Yes—oh, yes,' she said hurriedly. 'It's just...well,
you've made me far too pretty for one thing.'

'I painted you as I see you,' he declared. 'Apart from
the figure, of course,' he added quickly. 'That was pure
imagination.'

'That's obvious,' she said with a laugh, considerably embarrassed, 'because I'm afraid you'd find the reality deeply
disappointing.'

'Would I?'

His voice was husky and deep beside her ear, and she
swallowed hard. He was so close to her that she could feel
the heat from his body through her shirt. All she had to do
was turn. All she had to do was lean back...

No, Izzie, she told herself. You've made a complete fool
of yourself once already with this man. You're not about
to do it again.

'I'd better go,' she said, determinedly moving away from
him.

'Go?' he said in clear surprise.

'I've taken up more than enough of your time as it is,'
she pointed out, making for the landing.

'But what about your clothes?' he protested. 'They're
still in the washing machine—'

'You can return them to me tomorrow,' she declared as
she padded down the stairs, forcing him to follow her, but

when she reached the hall he cut in front of her and opened the sitting-room door.

'Izzie, would you come in here for a minute?'

'It's getting late—'

'Just for a minute—please?'

She didn't want to give him a minute. She didn't want to be here at all—in a house where she'd made such a fool of herself, wearing his clothes—but he looked so pleading that she found herself walking into the sitting room where she stopped with a frown.

'What happened to the painting?' she asked, noticing the blank wall above the fireplace.

'I decided it didn't look right there.'

Personally, she didn't think it would look right anywhere, but she didn't say that. Instead, she waited until he'd sat down on the settee then took the chair furthest away from him by the fire.

For a moment he said nothing, then he clenched his hands together tightly. 'Izzie, I want to tell you about Caroline.'

'Ben, it's OK,' she said quickly, not wanting to hear how wonderful his ex-wife had been. 'You don't have to explain. I know how much you loved Caroline—'

She came to a stunned halt. He'd started to laugh and she thought it was the most awful, bitter sound that she'd ever heard.

'Loved her?' he echoed harshly. 'Oh, yes, I loved her. In fact, a part of me still loved her even when she and her current boyfriend were killed in the car crash.'

'Her *current* boyfriend?' she gasped. 'But I thought—'

'So did everybody else at the beginning.' He nodded with an ironic smile. 'Lucky old Ben to have such a gorgeous young wife. Lucky old Ben to have Caroline to go home to. But it soon became poor old Ben when they discovered Caroline was never home because she was always in somebody else's bed.'

She couldn't bear to see the raw pain in his face and crossed the room quickly. 'Ben, you don't have to tell me this. I don't need to know—'

'You do,' he interrupted, his face drawn. 'You do, because I want you to understand.'

She didn't think she wanted to understand if it was going to cause him so much pain but, sensing his need to talk, she sat down beside him.

'All my friends tried to tell me what was going on,' he continued, his voice low, 'but I refused to believe it. My beautiful, wonderful Caroline couldn't be playing around, but when she became involved with my own SHO...' his lips twisted '...even I couldn't keep on pretending any more.'

'Was he the one who was killed in the car crash?' she asked quietly.

He nodded. 'They were coming back from a party and John was drunk. He lost control of the car on a bend and ploughed into a bridge. He was killed instantly. Caroline died three days later. It was when they carried out the post-mortem that I discovered Caroline was pregnant. And, before you ask, no, the child wasn't mine,' he continued, his voice tight. 'She wouldn't...she hadn't been letting me touch her for quite a long time.'

'Oh, Ben, why didn't you divorce her?' Izzie asked, longing to reach out and comfort him but knowing she mustn't. 'When you found out what she was like, why didn't you simply leave her?'

He stared bleakly at the blank wall above the fireplace for a long time before he answered. 'Because...because I didn't want to admit to myself what everyone knew already—that I was a failure as a husband.'

'But you weren't—'

'I was,' he insisted. 'If I hadn't married her, hadn't failed her, she'd still be alive today.'

'So you twisted her arm to marry you, did you?' she

flared. 'You dragged her, kicking and screaming, up the aisle?'

His lips curved slightly 'Actually, we were married in a registry office.'

'Oh, you know what I mean,' she protested. 'You can't make a woman marry you if she doesn't want to. Caroline was just a bitch.'

He shook his head. 'I should never have married her. I was wrong to think someone so outgoing and lively could ever be happy with someone like me.'

'But—'

'Izzie, I don't want you to feel sorry for me,' he interrupted, his face suddenly harsh. 'I've had enough pity from well-meaning friends to last me a lifetime. I just want you to know that I was a wash-out as a husband, and I've never been much of a prize in the romantic stakes, but every time I see you, every time I'm with you…'

He what? she wondered, but she didn't have time to ask because he suddenly reached out and cupped her face in his broad palms. Desperately she forced herself not to react, remembering only too clearly what had happened the last time she'd responded to his touch, but when he ran his thumb gently along her lower lip she got to her feet fast.

'I—I think I should go,' she stammered. 'It's getting late, and—'

'Izzie—will you stay?'

He'd spoken so quietly that she only just heard his soft entreaty. Was he asking her to do what she thought he was asking her to do? She didn't know and her eyes sought his.

'You…you mean you'd like some company?' she faltered.

He shook his head. 'Izzie, if you want to go home I'll take you home, but…'

'But what?' she asked through a throat so tight it hurt.

'I want…' A tide of dusky red advanced up his throat but he met her eyes squarely. 'Isabella, I know I have no right to ask this after the way I've treated you, but I want…' He paused and swallowed. 'God help me, but I want very much to make love to you.'

He hadn't said he loved her. He hadn't offered her any promise of a future together, but right now she didn't care. Right now all she was conscious of was the desperate need in his eyes and her own body's trembling response to it.

'Then I'll stay,' she whispered.

He let out the breath he must have been holding and the colour on his cheeks darkened to crimson. 'Izzie, there's something else you should know. I…I haven't done this for a long time.'

She smiled. A smile that was a little uneven, a little crooked round the edges. 'I've got a confession to make, too. I'm not exactly the world's greatest expert so maybe…maybe we could help each other?'

'It's a deal,' he said huskily.

And it was. Together they undressed each other, together they slipped beneath the duvet of his huge pine bed and together they caressed and explored one another until Izzie thought she would die with wanting him.

'Ben, please,' she gasped, tasting the salt sweat in the hollow of his throat, feeling his arms tremble as she wrapped her legs around him, urging, needing the final culmination.

He wanted it, too. She could feel it in the taut muscles of his back and thighs, could hear it in his ragged, uneven breathing, but it was almost as though he dreaded the final penetration, fearing that in some way he'd disappoint her.

'Ben…*please*,' she begged, lifting and pressing her hips against him so that he almost involuntarily slid home.

And then she didn't have to plead any more because the demands of Ben's own body took control, driving her onwards and onwards to a shattering release.

But when he reached his own climax only seconds after her, and his cry of elation matched her own, she didn't know whether it was tears or sweat that fell from his cheeks onto her breasts. All she knew as she gathered his shuddering body into her arms and held him tight was that she loved this man and always would.

CHAPTER NINE

MAYBE it was possible, Ben thought as he eased a stray lock of hair back from Izzie's forehead and heard her sigh in her sleep. Maybe people really did get a second chance at happiness. He'd never thought it was possible. He'd never believed it could happen to someone like him until he'd woken this morning to see Izzie curled up in bed beside him, her glorious hair spread out across his chest, her lips parted in a gentle smile.

His own lips curved as he stared down at her. For the first time in years he hadn't dreamt of Caroline. For the first time in years he hadn't woken feeling guilty, and it was all because of this girl. This girl who wasn't beautiful in the stunning, surface way that Caroline had been beautiful, but who was honest and genuine and real.

He glanced across at the clock on the bedside cabinet. They had a whole hour yet before they had to get up—a whole hour which, the lower part of his anatomy was urgently telling him, could be far better spent than dwelling on memories of his ex-wife.

Gently he eased the duvet down, wanting to admire again the rose-tipped splendour of Izzie's breasts. Even more gently he lightly brushed his finger across the top of one of them and felt the nipple harden instantly.

'Wake up, sleepyhead.' He chuckled as she muttered something unintelligible in her sleep.

'What is it?' she mumbled, opening her eyes slowly. 'Is something wrong?'

'Not one single, solitary thing,' he replied, his voice a low purr. 'In fact, I've just been thinking. For a couple of self-confessed amateurs, we did pretty well last night, didn't we?'

She laughed—a deep throaty sound that seemed to wrap itself around him.

'No regrets, then?' she asked, easing herself upright.

'None at all,' he replied. 'How about you?'

She shook her head. 'There's just one thing—'

Ben put his finger to her lips quickly. 'Hinny, there's so much I want to say to you, but right now—'

'It's too soon?' she suggested, her eyes large and dark.

He nodded. 'Caroline—she left me with a hell of a lot of hang-ups as well as guilt, and it's not easy for me to trust a woman again. I don't want you to think that last night was simply lust,' he added swiftly, seeing a slight frown crease her forehead, 'because it most certainly wasn't, but with Caroline everything happened so fast and this time I want to take things slowly.'

'I understand,' she murmured.

'And you must want that, too,' he said, scanning her face. 'After Steve, you must want to be completely sure this time.'

She wanted to tell him that she'd never been more certain of anything in her life, that the feelings she had for him were nothing like those she'd felt for Steve, but she was afraid he'd feel too pressurised if she did.

'We'll take things slowly,' she said instead.

Gently he lifted her hair from her shoulders and fanned it out through his fingers. 'You know, you have the most beautiful hair,' he murmured. 'It was the first thing I noticed about you.'

'Was it?' she said a little unsteadily. 'What was the second thing?'

A slow grin spread across his face. 'A pair of brown eyes that told me to go to the devil and a tongue that told me I was a prat.'

'Oh, don't,' she groaned, burying her face in his shoulder. 'The things I said to you...'

'I've been accused of a lot worse, believe me,' he said wryly. 'What was the first thing you noticed about me?'

She thought for a moment, then smiled. 'How tall you were, and then what a nice smile you had, and then...' Her smile deepened as she ran her fingers lightly through the dark hair on his chest. 'Then I spent an awful lot of time wondering whether this was as soft as it looked.'

'And is it?' he asked, his voice sounding slightly strangled.

'It sure is,' she said, planting a kiss there as though in confirmation and smiling secretly as she felt him tense. 'What time is it?' she continued, raising her head to look at him innocently.

'Just after six.'

'And we don't have to be at the hospital until eight,' she remarked thoughtfully. 'Which means we could either try to get some more sleep, or...'

'Or?' he prompted, his voice uneven.

Her eyes danced. 'We could have an early breakfast.'

'Breakfast?' he growled. 'Forget breakfast, woman. I've got a much better idea.'

'Really?' she exclaimed. 'What is it?'

He nudged his thigh against hers and she felt the hard evidence of his arousal.

'Why, Mr Farrell,' she said in mock amazement. 'Again?'

'But it's so much more satisfying than sleep or breakfast, don't you think?' he whispered huskily, lowering his head to tease one of her nipples with his tongue.

'Oh, yes,' she gasped, lying back on the pillow and clasping her hands around the back of his neck as he took the swollen nipple into his mouth. 'Oh, most definitely yes,' she added even more breathlessly when his fingers drifted slowly down her body, searching for and finally finding the all-too-betraying moisture of her own arousal.

'Oh, *damn*!' He swore as they both froze when they heard the shrill, insistent sound of his pager.

'It's one of the penalties of being a doctor, I'm afraid,' she said with a sigh as he rolled off her with a groan. 'When you've gotta go, you've just gotta go.'

'But does it have to be right now?' he protested as he wrenched the receiver off the phone and dialled the hospital.

His conversation was short and to the point and she didn't need him to tell her that it was serious.

'God knows when—or if—I'll be back,' he said as he got out of bed. 'With luck it might not take too long, but with an RTA—' He came to a halt and frowned. 'Just a minute. If I take the car, how are you going to get home?'

'I'll get the bus.'

'The *bus*!'

'I've been on one before, you know,' she pointed out as he gazed at her in horror. 'It's no big deal.'

'Maybe not,' he said, 'but it's not very romantic, is it? I mean, you give me the most fantastic night of my life and then you have to go home on a *bus*?'

She started to laugh, and after a second he joined her.

'I'll make it up to you, hinny, I promise,' he declared.

'Caviar and champagne next time?' She smiled.

'Whatever you want,' he answered, kissing her lightly on the forehead before padding across the bedroom to retrieve his clothes.

She couldn't prevent her eyes from following him. He was a striking-looking man fully dressed, but naked he was truly impressive. Covetously she charted the smooth planes of his neck and shoulders, the firm contours of his hips and thighs, but he must have sensed her scrutiny because he suddenly turned and smiled ruefully.

'Not fair, Isabella.'

'Now you know exactly what it feels like to be a woman and have a man ogle you.' She grinned cheekily.

'And is that what you're doing?' he murmured, his voice husky. 'Ogling me?'

'You bet,' she replied, deliberately running her tongue along her upper lip.

'Izzie, for God's sake, stop that,' he protested.

'Why?' she teased.

Wryly he glanced down at himself and then at her. 'I'd say that was pretty obvious, wouldn't you?'

It was. In fact, it was so very obvious that she blushed.

'Exactly.' He nodded. 'So, give me a break, huh?'

Obediently she stared primly up at the ceiling until he was dressed but when he left for the hospital, after having given her a lingering kiss and an even longer regretful sigh, she rolled onto her side and hugged her knees with a smile.

He'd made love to her twice during the night and each time it had been wonderful. Steve would have said that they'd simply had good sex but it was more than that— much more than that. She'd felt cherished. Cherished and safe and loved.

OK, so he hadn't actually said that he loved her. OK, so he'd said that he wanted to take things slowly, but if last night was an example of what he meant by taking things slowly then she'd vote for it any time.

She smiled again as she rolled back onto her pillow and then sighed as her eyes caught sight of the time. It was still early but she had no idea of the times of the buses back to Kelso and she supposed she ought to be making tracks.

A chuckle sprang from her as she got up. Ben had been horrified at the idea of her using public transport but, quite frankly, the way she was feeling this morning, she'd happily have walked home if she'd had to.

'Do you have to be so damned cheerful?' Fran snapped as Izzie began humming a song under her breath while she erased the name of the last patient they'd seen from the whiteboard. 'It's eleven o'clock in the morning, the place is heaving like it's a Saturday night after the pubs have shut and you're so damn cheerful it hurts.'

'Sorry.' Izzie grinned but Fran, she noticed, didn't.

In fact, now that Izzie really came to look at her, the staff nurse didn't look at all well.

'Are you OK, Fran?' she asked with concern.

'Of course I am,' she retorted. 'Look, I'm just having a bad day, that's all,' she continued more calmly as Izzie's eyebrows rose. 'Ignore me.'

'But—'

'And I don't think this department could stand another cheery soul this morning anyway,' Fran continued with a forced smile. 'Between you, Steve and Mr Farrell, we've already got a regular sunshine convention round here.'

'Steve's happy?' Izzie queried.

'Like a man who's just won the lottery.'

It was welcome news. For the past few weeks Steve had been uncharacteristically glum and today Izzie wanted everyone to be as happy as she was.

And she *was* happy—wildly, deliriously happy. All she needed to make her happiness complete was to see Ben again. Not to talk to him about last night, of course—she knew better than most how quickly rumours could fly around the Kelso General—but just to see him, perhaps to share a secret smile. But they'd been so busy since she'd come on duty that all she'd seen of him had been an occasional tantalising glimpse as he'd disappeared into the various cubicles.

With a sigh she washed her hands and lifted the sheaf of details April had handed through from Reception.

'Izzie, could I have a word?'

Steve was hovering behind her, an air of barely concealed excitement plain on his handsome face, and she smiled. 'Fire away.'

He opened his mouth and then shook his head as the doors to the treatment room opened and one of the porters wheeled in a stout, middle-aged woman.

'Later, OK, Izzie?' he muttered under his breath. 'I'll talk to you later. Now, then, Mrs…Mrs…?'

'Wallace,' the woman replied through pain-clenched teeth. 'Susan Wallace.'

'And what seems to be the trouble, Mrs Wallace?' Steve asked as Izzie helped the woman to her feet and into one of the cubicles.

'Pain,' she gasped. 'The most awful, awful pain. It started in my back a couple of hours ago, but now it seems to have moved to here.'

She was pointing to her groin, and as Izzie helped her off with her skirt Steve unrolled his stethoscope.

'Have you been sick at all, Mrs Wallace?'

'Twice. Once at home and once in the car.'

'And the pain you're experiencing?' Steve continued as Izzie attached the sphygmomanometer to Mrs Wallace's arm to take her blood pressure. 'Is it constant, or does it come and go?'

'It comes and goes. Please… Oh, please, can't you give me something to take it away?'

'In a moment,' Steve promised, 'but first we have to find out what's causing it. Have you noticed any problems lately when you've been passing urine?'

Mrs Wallace nodded. 'It's been more difficult to go, if you know what I mean.'

Gently Steve examined her stomach and groin, and then straightened up. 'It looks to me that you may have a kidney stone. A urine sample will confirm it, but I'm afraid you're going to have to be admitted.'

Mrs Wallace's face crumpled. 'You mean I'm going to have to have an operation?'

'We don't operate for kidney stones nowadays,' Steve replied. 'The first thing we'll do is give you plenty of fluid which should encourage the stone to pass through you naturally, but even if it doesn't we can remove it under a local anaesthetic by inserting a very narrow instrument into your bladder to crush the stone. The procedure's called a cystoscopy.'

'I don't care what it's called,' Mrs Wallace gasped with feeling, 'just so long as it gets rid of this pain.'

Quickly Steve made some notes. 'How much do you weigh, Mrs Wallace?'

'Weigh?' she repeated, puzzled.

Steve nodded. 'Your weight—what is it?'

'Um—ah—around ten stone?' she offered hopefully, but when Steve's eyebrows rose almost up to his hairline she managed a rueful smile. 'OK, OK, make that nearer twelve stone. And before you say anything,' she added as Steve opened his mouth, 'yes, I do know that I should go on a diet.'

'Dr Melville isn't being nosy, or deliberately asking an embarrassing question,' Izzie said gently as Steve filled a syringe with analgesic, 'but the painkillers we use are very powerful and how much we give you is determined by how much you weigh. If we get it wrong it could be very dangerous.'

'Rule number one, then, in a casualty department,' Mrs Wallace declared, wincing slightly as Steve inserted the syringe into her hip. 'Never lie about your weight to a doctor.'

'Never,' Izzie said, smiling.

With Mrs Wallace safely despatched to the wards, Izzie had just stripped the paper sheet off the trolley when Steve tapped her lightly on the shoulder.

'Got a minute now?' he asked.

The air of suppressed excitement still clung to him and her eyebrows rose. 'What's up?'

'Not here,' he replied mysteriously, ushering her quickly into their small dispensary, but when he closed the door she gave him a very hard stare and promptly opened it again.

'Steve, if this is some sort of practical joke—'

'No joke,' he interrupted, his eyes sparkling. 'I just wanted you to be the first to know. I got my exam results back this morning, Izzie, and I didn't just pass—I got distinction.'

'Oh, Steve, that's marvellous!' she exclaimed, hugging him with delight.

That was all she'd intended to do but Steve clearly had other ideas. The minute her arms were round him he clasped her tightly and began kissing her with a fervour that once would have had her melting in his arms. Once, but not any more.

'What the heck was that in aid of?' she demanded, half cross, half amused, when she finally managed to extricate herself from his grasp.

'Just reminding you of what you've been missing,' he grinned.

She tried to look severe but unfortunately an involuntary chuckle spoilt it.

'You're impossible—you know that, don't you?' she said.

'Of course,' he acknowledged cheekily, 'but passing my exams isn't my only news, Izzie. I've got another job—at the Metcalfe.'

'The Metcalfe?' she gasped, instantly recognising the name of one of London's most prestigious private hospitals. 'But when…? How?'

'I applied for the post three weeks ago and they offered it to me on condition that I passed my exams so I'm off to the big city in a month.'

'Boy, when you go for something, you really go for it, don't you?' she murmured, still stunned by his news.

'Come with me, Izzie.'

'C-come with you?' she stammered. 'But, Steve, I couldn't—'

'You can,' he insisted. 'The Metcalfe would welcome someone with your experience with open arms, and just think about it, Izzie. You'd be in London—the capital of Britain, the place where all the action is.'

She was thinking about it—the noise, the crowds, the loneliness of knowing no one.

'I'd never be happy in London, Steve,' she said slowly. 'I'm a country girl.'

'You'd be with me,' he said softly, and she sighed.

'Steve—'

'We had some good times together, didn't we?'

She couldn't deny it, and so she smiled. 'Yes, yes, we did.'

'And we could have some more,' he continued, his blue eyes fixed on her.

'No, we couldn't,' she said gently, not wanting to hurt him but knowing there was no other way. 'We don't want the same things any more, Steve. I don't think we ever did.'

'That's rubbish,' he protested. 'All I want from life is what everyone wants—to have fun.'

She stared at him thoughtfully. 'And what happens when the way you're living isn't fun any more?'

'You move on, of course—try something else.'

'Or someone else?' she suggested. 'I'm sorry, Steve,' she continued quickly as he opened his mouth, clearly intending to argue with her. 'Thanks for the offer, and thanks for caring enough about me to make it, but I can't go with you to London.'

Clear bewilderment appeared on his face for a second and then his blond eyebrows snapped together. 'It's Farrell, isn't it—you're stuck on Farrell?'

She blushed rosily despite all her best efforts not to. 'I like him, yes—'

'I thought he and sex on legs were an item?' he interrupted.

'Sex on legs?' she repeated in confusion.

'The redhead with the green eyes—Joanna Ogilvy.'

She chuckled. 'Ben only went out with her once.'

'That's not what I heard,' he said.

'I don't care what you heard,' she said with irritation. 'It's what I know.'

'If you say so.' He turned to go and then paused, curiosity plain on his face. 'Just tell me one thing, Izzie. What's Farrell got that I haven't?'

She shook her head. 'You wouldn't understand.'

'Try me.'

She looked at him for a moment and then smiled. 'Would you believe—a great deal of kindness?'

He stared back at her, obviously deeply puzzled, and then shrugged. 'OK, fine. If you don't want to tell me, don't.'

'But I just have,' she protested.

'Yeah, right, and I was born yesterday,' he scoffed. 'If he's what you want, Izzie, then good luck to you, but I hope you know what you're doing.'

She did know what she was doing, she thought as she followed him out of the dispensary. In fact, she'd never been more certain of anything in her life. She only wished she could tell someone how happy she was. Fran, for one, looked in serious need of cheering up but she knew she mustn't tell anyone, not now, not yet.

'We have a waiting room full of patients, Sister Clark,' a deep voice suddenly snapped in her ear, 'a waiting room that isn't going to get any emptier while you stand around, admiring the scenery.'

'Sorry?' she spluttered, turning round to find Ben gazing down at her, his grey eyes as cold and as unyielding as granite.

'And so you should be,' he continued tightly. 'If you

have nothing better to do—and you quite plainly haven't—I'd welcome a little assistance in 2.'

What on earth was that in aid of? she wondered, as he strode away. It was the first time he'd spoken to her all morning. Though she hadn't expected any favouritism, what she certainly hadn't expected was a lambasting.

Maybe he's had a bad morning, she told herself as she helped him calm down the terrified parents of a three-year-old who had swallowed some sleeping pills. Maybe he's simply trying to be discreet, she kept telling herself as the day wore on, but by mid-afternoon, when every word she uttered resulted in either icy sarcasm or a comprehensive snub, even she had to admit that there was a vast difference between discretion and being quite appallingly rude.

'Boy, but he's a real pain in the butt today.' Fran grimaced after she and Izzie had helped Ben suture the badly lacerated leg of one of the local farmers who had impaled himself on a pitchfork. 'And he's really got it in for you, hasn't he? I thought the two of you might get it together eventually but there's fat chance of that happening by the look of things.'

But they had got it together, Izzie thought unhappily as Fran disappeared into Reception. Last night they had most definitely got it together. What had happened since to make him treat her this way? What on earth had occurred to cause the man who only a few hours ago had whispered such heart-stopping sweet nothings into her ear to treat her with such contempt?

'Another patient for you, Sister.' One of the porters beamed, interrupting her thoughts as he wheeled a familiar-looking figure towards her.

'Oh, Mrs Anderson,' Izzie exclaimed in dismay, 'you haven't fallen and hurt yourself again, have you?'

'No, she hasn't,' the tall, distinguished-looking man with her replied, 'but you've really got to do something about her arm, Sister. My wife's not a wimp—in fact, I'd say

Grace can stand a whole lot more pain than I can—but this last week—'

'It's been a nightmare,' Mrs Anderson tearfully completed for her husband. 'I know the doctor said I was only to come back if I felt pins and needles in my arm, or if my fingers turned blue, but I just can't take this pain. I really can't.'

'What sort of pain is it?' Izzie asked, kneeling down in front of her and noting the pallor of Mrs Anderson's cheeks, the beads of sweat shimmering on her forehead. 'A stabbing one, a grumbling one?'

'It's as though someone's digging a red-hot poker into me,' Mrs Anderson replied convulsively. 'Not just once, but over and over again.'

'Please, don't upset yourself,' Izzie said gently as large tears began to roll down Mrs Anderson's ashen cheeks. 'I'll get a doctor to see you, and I'm sure you'll soon be fine.'

But neither Ben nor Steve was free. Ben was dealing with a spinal injury, and Steve was trying to calm down a terrified teenager who was hyperventilating. Both of them looked as though they were going to be some time and the last thing Izzie wanted was to prolong Mrs Anderson's agony. Quickly she beckoned to Tess.

'Would you take Mrs Anderson along to the plaster room for me, Tess, and tell them to cut off her cast? I think she may have a trapped nerve, or she could have sustained another break, but either way that cast's got to come off to find out what's causing such pain.'

The student nurse nodded, half turned to go and then came forward a step. 'Sister, could I have a word with you?'

'Don't tell me you've got a job at the Metcalfe too?' Izzie chuckled and then shook her head as Tess gazed blankly at her. 'Skip it. What can I do for you?'

'It isn't me,' she replied, coming forward another step

and deliberately lowering her voice. 'It's Staff Nurse Walton. She's in the staffroom, and she's crying.'

Izzie gazed at the student nurse in disbelief. Fran never cried. She might have been known to wipe her eyes surreptitiously after they'd dealt with a particularly harrowing case, but to cry…

And Fran wasn't simply crying, as Izzie discovered after she'd sent Tess off with Mrs Anderson, she was breaking her heart.

'It's David Renton,' Fran sobbed in answer to Izzie's gentle questioning. 'The fireman who was hurt in the fire at Houndslow's. He's dead. I just heard he died an hour ago.'

'And you knew him?' Izzie said with dawning comprehension.

'*Knew* him?' Fran cried wretchedly. 'Izzie, he was best man at our wedding—he and his wife, Rhona, are amongst our closest friends. And the awful thing—the truly awful thing—is that all I keep thinking is thank God it's not Jim.'

'Oh, Fran—'

'I feel so guilty,' the staff nurse said with a hiccup. 'David and Rhona—they've got two lovely little boys— and all I can think of is myself. What kind of woman am I? What kind of bitch have I become?'

'Fran, stop it,' Izzie said firmly. 'What you're feeling… It isn't wicked, or uncaring—it's normal. No matter how close you are to your friends, your husband and your family will always come first. It's human nature.'

'Then you don't think I'm a heartless cow?' Fran faltered.

'Of course I don't,' Izzie exclaimed. 'If I loved someone—truly loved someone—then I'm afraid I'd consider the whole world well lost so long as that person was all right.'

'You really mean that, don't you?' Fran said thoughtfully, her own distress temporarily forgotten.

Unconsciously Izzie's face softened. 'Yes, yes, I do.'

'Izzie, about Mr Farrell—'

'Forget about Mr Farrell,' she interrupted quickly, seeing the speculative look in Fran's eyes. 'What you need is to wash your face, put your feet up and have a nice cup of tea.'

'But we're so busy—'

'We'll cope.'

'But—'

'Hey, who's the sister round here—you or me?' Izzie asked with mock severity as she switched on the kettle. 'Do as you're told, Staff Nurse Walton.'

Fran managed to smile but as Izzie walked slowly back down the corridor towards the treatment room her face was pensive. She'd meant what she'd said to Fran. Just the thought of Ben being hurt, far less killed, was enough to make her stomach knot into a hard ball of pain. It didn't matter that he'd been horrible to her all day. If anything were to happen to him she knew it would feel as though her heart were being torn out.

'I'd like a word with you, Sister Clark.'

That had to be everyone's opening gambit today, she decided with a smile as she turned to face Ben. Her smile died instantly. Never had she seen him looking quite so angry, and her heart sank.

'Something I can do for you?' she asked.

'Who authorised the removal of Mrs Anderson's cast?'

'I beg your pardon?' she answered in confusion.

'As well you might,' he said icily, 'but that still doesn't answer my question. Who authorised the removal of Mrs Anderson's cast?'

'No one did,' she began, 'but I thought—'

'You are not paid to think, Sister Clark.'

Her jaw dropped. '*What* did you say?'

'You heard me,' he continued, his face an expressionless

mask. 'You're a nurse who's paid to nurse, not to diagnose.'

The injustice of his remark cut her to the quick but her
head came up defiantly. 'I'm sorry that you feel I exceeded
my authority, Mr Farrell, but both you and Dr Melville
were busy and Mrs Anderson was in agony. What course
of treatment would you have authorised?'

A faint flush of colour appeared on his cheeks. 'That's
not the point.'

No, of course it wasn't, she thought angrily, because they
both knew damn well that she'd done exactly what he
would have ordered if he'd been asked.

'Then what is the point?' she asked, her tone every bit
as cold as his.

'Where's Staff Nurse Walton?' he demanded, deliberately ignoring her question.

'She's upset. I've told her to have a cup of tea.'

'Ah, yes, tea,' he sneered. 'Your universal panacea for
all ills. Well, once she's enjoyed this leisurely cup of tea I
want her back on duty. A and E has no room for passen-
gers.'

'She will come back on duty when—and if—I decide
she's fit to do so,' she retorted. 'Fran has just heard that a
very good friend of hers has died and I think even you
might allow her a little time to recover from that.'

The colour on his cheeks darkened to crimson. 'I'm
sorry, I didn't know—'

'Then perhaps in future you should think before you
jump to conclusions.'

'I hardly think you're in any position to make moral
judgements, do you?' he snapped back.

She gazed up at him, stunned. 'And what the hell is that
supposed to mean?'

He didn't even answer. He just banged through the doors
into Reception, and her chin came up. She'd had enough.

There was only so much any woman could take and she'd reached her limit.

'OK, I want some answers from you, and I want them right now,' she exploded when she caught up with him at the exit to A and E. 'What the hell's going on?'

His eyebrows rose. 'Going on?'

'You know damn well what I mean,' she hissed back at him under her breath, all too aware of the people who were passing. 'Last night...this morning, you said, you implied—'

'I'm surprised you can even remember last night,' he interrupted tightly. 'Don't these one-night stands get confusing?'

For a second she gazed up at him in hurt bewilderment and then shook her head. 'I'm not even going to dignify that with an answer—especially as I don't know what the hell you're talking about.'

'Then let me enlighten you,' he said, his eyes cold. 'Call me old-fashioned but I consider commitment to be an important part of a relationship, and it sure as hell isn't my idea of commitment to find you in the arms of another man just a few hours after we've made love.'

'In the arms of another man?' she echoed in confusion, and then suddenly she realised what had happened. He must have seen Steve kissing her and thought... 'Oh, Ben you idiot! What you saw—it's not what you think. I was congratulating Steve on his exam results, that's all.'

'Really?' he declared, his lip curling. 'Maybe I should take a few if that's the reaction it merits.'

'Ben, you're getting this all wrong,' she protested, annoyingly aware that she was blushing—not from guilt but from anger. 'You're jumping to conclusions again—'

'No, I'm not,' he interrupted, his face hard. 'In fact, I'm just beginning to understand. Last night was simply a pathetic attempt to make Steve jealous, wasn't it?'

'Of course it wasn't!' she flared. 'How can you even think such a thing?'

'Because I had a very good teacher,' he said bitingly. 'Caroline used to play exactly the same game and, believe me, you're an amateur in comparison.'

'Ben, listen to me—'

'There's such a thing as trust, Izzie.'

'That's exactly what I'm thinking,' she said, her face suddenly hard, 'and yet you seem awfully anxious to judge and condemn me.'

'What the hell did you expect when I saw you in Steve's arms?' he demanded.

'That you might ask me for an explanation, before condemning me,' she said quietly.

Indecision appeared on his face—indecision and uncertainty—and then his jaw hardened. 'I'm sorry, Izzie, but I've been through all this with Caroline and I don't want to go through it again. And now I must go,' he continued as she opened her mouth to protest. 'I've got a date.'

'A date?' she repeated faintly.

He gestured towards the car park and she saw a familiar figure standing beside his car.

'You're going out with *Joanna*?' she gasped.

'At least she doesn't pretend to be something she's not,' he said grimly, seeing the hurt in her eyes. 'At least she's honest about what she wants.'

She stared at him for a long moment and then shook her head. 'If you believe that, Ben Farrell, then you really are a fool.'

And she turned on her heel and walked away without a backward glance.

CHAPTER TEN

THE hairdresser's eyes met Izzie's in the mirror with dismay. 'You want your hair cut into a short bob?'

'That's right.'

'But, madam, your hair's far too curly for that style. It won't ever stay flat.'

'I don't care.'

'What about something a little longer?' the hairdresser suggested. 'Shoulder-length could be very flattering.'

'I don't want it shoulder-length,' Izzie declared. 'I want it cut really short. To here,' she added, placing the back of her hand up against her ear in demonstration. 'In a bob.'

'But, madam—'

'Cut it.'

'But—'

'Cut it,' Izzie repeated in a tone that brooked no opposition, and the hairdresser reached for her scissors with a sigh.

One look at Fran's stunned expression when Izzie crept into the A and E staffroom just before the start of their Saturday night shift was enough to confirm Izzie's worst suspicions.

'It's dreadful, isn't it?' She sighed as the staff nurse opened her mouth then closed it again quickly.

'Of course it's not,' Fran replied loyally. 'It's... different.'

Izzie stared unhappily at her reflection in the staffroom mirror and shook her head. 'It's a mess. The hairdresser warned me that my hair was too curly but I never thought it would look like this. Dammit, you'd think I'd stuck my finger in a light socket.'

Fran started to laugh, then tactfully converted her laughter into a cough when she saw Izzie's miserable expression. 'A little mousse might help, some gel…'

'Frankly, I'd say a paper bag's the only answer to this,' Izzie groaned, tugging at the ends of her hair in a vain attempt to make them appear longer.

'What on earth made you decide to get it cut in the first place?' Fran demanded as she put her handbag into the cupboard. 'You swore after that disastrous urchin cut you had five years ago that you'd never do it again.'

Because my hair is the one thing Ben ever raved about, Izzie answered mentally. Because every time I looked in the mirror I could picture his hands running through it. Because in some stupid, masochistic way I'm hoping he's going to be horrified when he sees it.

But she didn't tell Fran any of that. Instead she simply shrugged. 'I felt like a change.'

'I wonder what Mr Farrell's going to think of this change?' Fran asked, shooting her a thoughtful glance.

'I couldn't care less,' Izzie replied tartly. 'What I do to my hair is none of his business. In fact, nothing I do is any of his business.'

Fran gazed at her speculatively for a moment, then sighed. 'If you say so.'

'I do say so,' Izzie insisted, uncomfortably aware from Fran's expression that she was protesting too much. 'And now we'd better get ourselves out on duty,' she continued quickly. 'It's almost eight o'clock and I don't want to be late.'

In truth, she didn't care whether she was late or not, she realised as she left the staffroom. Once she'd loved coming to work, had relished the challenges her job had brought, but not any more. Now each day was simply something to be endured, and it was all because of Ben Farrell. Ben

Farrell, who'd somehow made her fall in love with him and yet who'd spent the last two weeks virtually ignoring her.

'Izzie!'

Well, at least it was an improvement on the coldly polite 'Sister Clark' she'd been enduring for the past fortnight, she decided as she looked up to see Ben walking down the corridor towards her, and his stunned expression was all she could have wished for.

'Your hair!' he exclaimed. 'What have you done to your hair?'

'Do you like it?' she asked, deliberately turning round so he could see the back in all its hideous glory.

'Why, Izzie?' he asked quietly, his grey eyes fixed on her. 'Why did you do it?'

'Why not?' she challenged, but he didn't say anything.

He simply stared down at her and she found herself thinking that she'd never seen him looking quite so tired and drawn. Of course he looks tired and drawn, her mind said sharply. He's dating Joanna, isn't he? and I doubt if she's allowing him much sleep.

'Look, I don't have to explain my actions to you,' she declared, all too conscious that she was perilously close to doing exactly that. 'It's my hair—I can do whatever I want with it.'

Still he said nothing, and her chin came up a notch.

'You obviously hate it so why don't you just say so?' she demanded.

He half stretched out his hand to her and for one wonderful, heart-stopping moment she thought he was actually going to touch her shorn curls, then his hand fell to his side.

'No, I don't hate it,' he murmured with a slightly crooked smile. 'I can't deny I preferred it longer, but I'll always think you have beautiful hair, Isabella.'

Why did he have to say that? she wondered as her heart twisted inside her. Why did he have to be kind? She didn't want him to be kind. She wanted him angry or upset—anything but kind.

'It's a matter of complete indifference to me what you think,' she managed to say tightly.

Without waiting for his reply, she strode down the corridor, her back straight, her head held high, but her defiance lasted only until she was safely inside the treatment room. She couldn't go on like this, and she knew it. If she could have hated him it would have been different, but she didn't hate him. No matter how much he'd hurt her she still loved him, but she knew, after Caroline, that he was never going to trust her enough to return her love.

So, what do you do now, Izzie? her heart asked. There's only one thing I can do, she answered sadly. I'll have to leave the General. I can't stay on here, seeing him day after day, feeling as though my heart is breaking into pieces little by little. I can't spend the rest of my life watching him shooting out of A and E every evening, knowing he's going to Joanna.

She had to find herself a new job but it wouldn't be easy and it would take time. Not necessarily, she suddenly realised as she noticed Steve standing by the whiteboard. Quickly she made her way towards him.

'Of course I can still get you a job at the Metcalfe,' he said after he'd ribbed her mercilessly about her hair. 'All I need to do is lift the phone and the job's as good as yours. So, do you want me to fix it for you?'

For a second she hesitated. Ben had followed her into the treatment room and was watching her, his features harsh under the fluorescent lighting. Perhaps I should wait a little longer, her heart whispered. Perhaps he'll realise he's wrong, that he can trust me. And what if he doesn't? her mind countered. What if all you can ever have of him is what you have right now?

Steve was waiting expectantly for her answer and she

took a deep breath. 'Yes,' she said. 'Yes, I want you to fix it for me.'

'Brilliant!' he exclaimed with delight. 'And you won't regret it, Izzie. I promise you won't.'

She didn't know whether she would or not, but as she watched him walk jauntily away she knew there was no going back.

By ten o'clock the thought of working in a private hospital like the Metcalfe had become infinitely more appealing.

'God knows what it's going to be like in here when the pubs shut,' Fran winced as the decibel level from Reception increased. 'It already sounds as though there's a riot going on out there.'

Izzie grimaced in agreement. The Kelso General might not deal with the same volume of patients as a large city hospital but weekends were always busy and far too many of their casualties were there because of drink-related accidents.

'Somebody really ought to have a word with Mavis,' Fran continued as she binned the swabs they'd been using on their last patient. 'She's out in Reception again and, frankly, I'd say it was the last place she should be on a Saturday night.'

Izzie couldn't agree more but she doubted whether Mavis would listen to their concern, and she didn't.

'These young lads don't worry me, dear,' the old lady replied, after Izzie had taken her into one of their private waiting rooms. 'They're only full of high spirits.'

I'll bear that in mind the next time one of the young layabouts throws up all over me, Izzie thought wryly, but she knew better than to press the matter. Mavis might look as though a puff of wind would blow her over but she had an iron will and if Izzie forced her into a corner she'd undoubtedly set up residence in Reception every Saturday night just to be contrary.

There was something else she wanted to talk to her about anyway, something she was convinced Mavis would be only too delighted to hear.

'I remembered you told me you used to be a nurse,' she said as she bought the old lady a coffee from the drinks dispenser, 'so I had a word with the local WVS about you. Apparently, they're desperately short of volunteers to visit patients whose families live too far away to make regular visits practicable.'

'And?' Mavis asked, her faded brown eyes fixed on her.

'I told them I was sure you'd be only too happy to volunteer,' Izzie said with a smile.

Mavis put down her coffee. 'Then you can just un-tell them.'

'Un-tell them?' Izzie exclaimed, totally thrown. 'But I thought—'

'I know what you thought,' the old lady interrupted firmly. 'You thought that if you got me a job it would give me a reason to get up in the morning, and I'd feel fulfilled and all that sort of psychological claptrap. Well, I'm sorry to disappoint you, but this isn't the movies where a kind-hearted nurse solves everybody's problems in the last reel. This is real life and, though you may not approve of the way I live, I like my life exactly the way it is.'

Izzie flushed scarlet. 'I'm sorry—I never meant you to think I was interfering, butting in—'

'I know you didn't,' Mavis said, reaching out to pat Izzie's hand gently. 'Look, you're a nice girl, and your heart's in the right place—'

'Do you know something, Mavis?' Izzie broke in vexedly. 'I'm heartily sick to death of people telling me that I'm a nice girl, especially when I know damn well that what they actually mean is I've got about as much sex appeal as a boiled potato!'

Mavis's eyebrows rose and then a smile appeared on her lips. 'You've had a row with Mr Farrell, haven't you?'

Izzie started to protest, to deny it, but when the smile on the old lady's lips deepened she gave up. 'You could say that. He's decided that he prefers the company of a red-headed siren with the looks of Helen of Troy and the sex appeal of a page-three girl.'

A frown appeared on Mavis's forehead. 'I take it this bimbo's petite and dainty and flutters her eyelashes a lot?'

'She is and she does.'

'And unfortunately you look so damn capable. No offence meant, dear,' she added quickly as a wry smile appeared on Izzie's face.

'None taken.'

Mavis's frown deepened. 'I don't suppose... You couldn't make yourself look a bit more vulnerable, could you?'

'With my height?' Izzie protested.

'I see what you mean,' Mavis said, gazing critically up at her, 'but don't give in without a fight. I did that many years ago and lived to regret it. It's all water under the bridge for me now,' she continued as Izzie's eyebrows rose questioningly, 'but you've still got a chance to put it right.'

'I've already made a start,' Izzie said briskly. 'I've decided to leave the General.'

Mavis's small face creased in dismay and she shook her head. 'Bad move, dear.'

'I'd say it was the only move I can make,' Izzie replied.

And it was, she told herself as she walked back into the treatment room.

Staying on at the General, that was a recipe for disaster, and as for Mavis's advice... How could someone who was five feet eleven and weighed ten and a half stones on a good day make herself look vulnerable? The very idea was enough to bring a smile to her lips.

'Care to share the joke?' a deep voice murmured behind her.

Her smiled died instantly, and her expression when she

turned was coolly professional. 'I don't think you'd appreciate the humour, Mr Farrell.'

His eyes caught and held hers. 'You used to call me Ben,' he said softly.

And you called me hinny when we made love, she thought, but not for the world would she ever remind him of it.

'Is there something I can do for you, Mr Farrell?' she asked, deliberately ignoring his comment as she reached for the list of waiting casualties that April had sent through from Reception. 'As you can see, I'm very busy.'

To her surprise he looked awkward, uncomfortable. 'I just… I simply wondered how you were, that's all.'

Anyone would think she was suffering from some dreadful, debilitating disease, she thought angrily, but, then, maybe that was how he viewed the night they'd spent together. As something to be talked about in hushed, embarrassed tones.

'Worried that I might be pregnant, are you?' she said tartly. 'If I am you can always blame it on Steve.'

He winced as she walked away but she didn't care. She'd had enough of being a nice girl, enough of being a doormat who took anything and everything anyone cared to dish out. From now on she was going to look out for herself and if that meant hurting people then so be it.

Tess was clearly in the same frame of mind as she bounced down the treatment room, her small face angry.

'Sometimes I wonder why we bother,' she said furiously. 'I've just spent the better part of an hour picking the remains of a broken bottle out of a woman's arm, and do I get any thanks? No, I don't. I get a string of abuse because the drunken idiot's had to wait for half an hour in Reception.'

'I think it's called having a vocation,' Izzie said drily.

'I think I need my head examined,' the student replied

with feeling, and Izzie laughed as she headed off to the staffroom to snatch a cup of tea.

But her hopes of enjoying it in peace and quiet were quickly dashed. Within seconds of her switching on the kettle Ben appeared at the door, and one glance at his face told her he was in a foul mood.

'Tea or coffee?' she asked, holding up both jars.

'What's all this nonsense I hear about you leaving the General?' he said without preamble, his face grim.

Steve and his big mouth, she thought with irritation as she popped two teabags in the teapot.

'It's not nonsense,' she said calmly. 'I've decided I need a change.'

'Izzie, you can't,' he protested, thrusting his hands through his black hair angrily. 'You can't go running after a man like Steve—a man who'll use you, hurt you.'

He's got a nerve, she thought, switching the kettle off with a snap. If anyone had really hurt her, it was him.

'Milk and sugar?' she said, her voice barely civil as she retrieved two mugs from the cupboard.

'I won't let you do this,' he exclaimed, yanking the mugs from her fingers and banging them down on the small work surface. 'I won't let you muck up your life.'

'Oh, you won't, will you?' she retorted, her expression every bit as angry as his. 'And how—exactly—do you propose to stop me?'

'Izzie—Izzie, you must listen to me,' he said, his colour high. 'That day when I saw you with Steve, I think I may have made a mistake. I think I may have been a bit too hasty.'

'You *think* you may have made a mistake?' she said, incensed. 'You *think* you may have been a bit too hasty? Well, pardon me if I don't break out into a round of applause at your new-found insight. What's caused this revelation?' she continued as he tried to interrupt. 'Discovered

Joanna's a lying, conniving bitch, have you, and now you figure good old Izzie's better than no one?'

'No!' he declared, his cheeks reddening still further. 'Look, I'm obviously not phrasing this very well—'

'Oh, I think you're phrasing it perfectly,' she retorted, 'and I've got news for you, Mr Farrell. Good old Izzie's nobody's second best, and she's nobody's fool.'

'Izzie, wait—'

But she didn't wait. She simply pushed past him and kept on going until she reached the treatment room.

'That was a very fast teabreak,' Tess observed in surprise when she saw her.

'I decided I wasn't thirsty,' Izzie replied. 'Right, who's next?' she added quickly as the student nurse's eyebrows rose in clear curiosity.

Tess grimaced. 'A right little charmer called Robbie Lang. According to him, he slipped and fell on something sharp down by the river. My guess is he's been in a fight.'

It was Izzie's guess, too, as the young man came swaggering through into the treatment area. The slight wound on his arm could have been caused by anything, but the bruises on his chest and face could only have been caused by blows.

'Wanna take my trousers off too, darlin'?' He leered as she eased off his bloodstained shirt. 'I'm sure you'll find the scenery down there a hell of a lot more interesting than my arm.'

'That won't be necessary, Mr Lang,' she replied evenly, reaching for some swabs.

'Oh, I like that,' he said with a laugh, sprawling back over the trolley in what she presumed he considered a provocative pose. '*Mr* Lang. I like tarts who are polite.' His eyes dropped to her breasts. 'Not to mention tarts who have a pair on them, begging to be squeezed.'

And he did just that.

Involuntarily her hand clenched into a tight fist and she

relaxed it with difficulty. Never rise to the bait, she reminded herself. No matter what the provocation, never rise
to the bait—it only encourages antagonism.

'I'd rather you didn't do that, Mr Lang,' she said with a
calmness she was very far from feeling. 'Not while I'm
holding a pair of scissors.'

'Oh, come on, sweetheart,' he urged, running a none too
clean hand up her bare arm. 'I know what you nurses are
like, and you're not a bad looker.'

And you're really pathetic, she thought, picking up another swab. Robbie Lang couldn't have been any more than
nineteen or twenty, and yet already she could see the marks
of heavy drinking on his face.

'Do you suffer from any allergies, Mr Lang?'

'Wouldn't know, darlin'.'

'Any history of heart disease, high blood pressure—?'

'How about a date?' he interrupted.

'I don't think so,' she replied, and then gasped in pain
as he grasped her tightly by the wrist.

'Not good enough for you, eh?' he flared, pushing his
face close up to hers. 'Think you're a cut above me, do
you, you stuck-up bitch?'

She could smell the cheap spirits on his breath, could
see that his face was contorted with furious anger, but what
she was most concerned about was the deathly hush that
had suddenly descended outside the cubicle. Please, don't
let anyone come in, she prayed. Robbie was unpredictable
enough, without having a bigger audience to play to, but
her prayer went unanswered. The cubicle curtains suddenly
opened behind her, and Ben was there.

'Having trouble, Sister Clark?' he asked, his expression
tight.

'Nothing I can't handle, Mr Farrell,' she replied
smoothly, willing him to turn round and go out again, but
he didn't. In fact, he simply moved closer to her, if anything.

'This your boyfriend, darlin'?' the young man asked, gazing up at Ben critically. 'Bit old for you, isn't he?'

'If you'd let go of my wrist for a moment, Mr Lang, I'd like to give you a tetanus injection,' she declared, deliberately ignoring his jibe.

'If you really are her boyfriend,' Robbie continued, tightening his grip still further, 'you must know what her boobs looks like. Big, are they? They sure felt big.'

Izzie groaned inwardly. Ben was losing his temper. She could see it in the tightening of his jaw, the hardening of his eyes, and it was the last thing she wanted or needed. At the moment Robbie Lang was merely full of drunken bravado, but if Ben gave him a focus for his aggression they could have a very nasty situation indeed.

'I'm sure there must be other casualties needing your attention, Mr Farrell,' she said quickly. 'I can manage here.'

But Ben didn't even look in her direction. His gaze stayed fixed on Robbie Lang's face.

'Take your grubby little hand off Sister Clark,' he said, his voice ice-cold. 'And take it off *now*!'

'Ooh—big talk from the big man!' Robbie taunted, pulling Izzie closer. 'And what you gonna do if I don't, pal?'

'Punch you from here to kingdom come, *pal*,' Ben snapped.

The young man's eyes narrowed for a second and then, before either Ben or Izzie could move, an old-fashioned razor suddenly appeared in his hand, its blade gleaming ominously under the treatment-room lights.

'I don't think so,' Robbie murmured silkily as he got to his feet. 'I don't think so unless you want your girlfriend's face permanently rearranged.'

'Mr Lang,' Izzie began. 'Robbie—'

'Trying to be nice to me now, eh, darlin'?' he sneered, waving the razor at her. 'Well, it's too late because—'

The rest of what he'd been about to say died on his lips

as Ben lunged at him. Momentarily diverted, Robbie's hold on Izzie slackened and she pulled herself free from his grasp, only to see the razor pass horrifyingly close to Ben's chest as he attempted to wrest it from Robbie's fingers. Anger and fear gave her trembling legs impetus and she threw herself forward just as Ben's fist made contact with Robbie's chin.

Robbie let out a roar of expletives as he crashed to the floor and the cubicle seemed suddenly to be full of people, but all Izzie was aware of was Ben's arms holding her tight.

'You idiot—you idiot!' she choked into his chest, terror making her angry. 'I had everything under control until you decided to do your macho-man act. Don't you realise he could have killed you?'

'It would take considerably more than one young thug to get the better of me,' he said soothingly, but she refused to be placated.

'Don't ever do anything like that again,' she exclaimed, pulling herself free from his arms slightly. 'Promise me that you won't ever—'

She came to a halt. She felt sick and not a little dizzy, but that wasn't what had made her bereft of speech. It was the large red stain that she could see across the front of Ben's white coat.

'Oh, my God, you *are* hurt! Take off your jacket... Sit down... Steve—where's Steve?' she demanded, gazing wildly round at the sea of faces that surrounded them. 'For God's sake, somebody do something. Can't you see Ben's hurt, that he needs—'

'Izzie...Izzie, it isn't my blood,' Ben interrupted, his eyes suddenly wide with fear. 'It's yours.'

'Mine?' she said, staring down at herself in disbelief. 'But it can't be mine...it can't...'

But it was, and as the world suddenly began to tilt and go dark, and Ben's voice seemed to become fainter and fainter in her ears, all she could think was, Mavis, when

you suggested I should try to look vulnerable I don't think
you meant I should get myself killed.

'Ben, this is ridiculous,' Izzie protested as he drew his car
to a halt outside his cottage. 'Mr Evanton said I fainted
because of shock, not because I was badly hurt. The cut
didn't even need stitches, just steri-strips.'

'Evanton also said that you should stay in hospital over-
night,' he replied as he helped her out of the car, 'but as
you refused you're staying with me so that I can keep an
eye on you.'

'But—'

'Izzie, I'm not going to argue with you,' he interrupted,
steering her firmly but gently down the path. 'You're here,
and you're going to stay here if I have to padlock you to
a seat.'

A shaky chuckle broke from her but in truth the gash
that Robbie had inflicted just below her collar-bone hurt a
great deal more than she cared to admit, and to have someone take care of her, fuss over her, was wonderful. Or at
least it would have been wonderful if the person doing it
hadn't been Ben Farrell.

'You don't have to do this, you know,' she said as he
led her into the sitting room and settled her on the couch.
'Just because we…because you and I… You don't owe me
anything.'

He sat down beside her and trapped her hands firmly in
his. 'I do. I owe you a great deal more than I'll ever be
able to repay. Izzie, listen to me. I'm not very good with
words. I can't make up flowery speeches or utter extrava-
gant compliments but when you collapsed onto the floor of
A and E…when I saw the blood and thought what my life
would be like without you…' He paused and smiled ruefully. 'Look, I guess what I'm trying to say is I love you.'

'B-but what about Joanna?' she stammered in amazement. 'You said she was your kind of girl. You said—'

'Izzie, I've been out with the damn woman twice, and believe me, it was twice too often.'

'Twice?' she echoed. 'But, Ben, she's so beautiful, so petite—'

'And one big pain in the butt,' he finished for her wryly. 'Izzie, I think I fell in love with you the first day we met. I know I love you now, and I always will.'

His eyes were fixed on her with such intensity that she had difficulty meeting them. 'For a man who's supposed to be not very good with words,' she murmured a little shakily, 'I'd say you were doing pretty well.'

A fleeting smile curved his lips. 'You told me I was a fool, and I am. You're the best thing that's ever happened to me, and I'm not going to let you go off with Steve without a fight. Don't tell me I've left it too late,' he continued as she opened her mouth to protest that she had absolutely no intention of going anywhere with Steve, 'because I won't accept it.'

'Ben—'

'I know I've got my fair share of hang-ups after Caroline. I know I won't be the easiest man in the world to live with, but will you marry me, Izzie? I know I'm not the world's greatest catch but can you…do you think you might be able to love me?'

Hope and fear were equally mixed on his face. It wouldn't be easy to be married to him. His pride had been badly hurt and she sensed that it would take a long time for him to get that pride back, but she wanted to give him that time—oh, how much she wanted to give him that time.

'Ben, I already love you,' she whispered, 'and I'll marry you tomorrow if you really want me to.'

He gazed down at her blankly and for a moment she wondered if he'd changed his mind, then he stood up with a smile that was blinding.

'*If* I want you?' he uttered. '*If?*'

He pulled her into his arms in a crushing embrace and she let out a yelp of pain.

'I'm sorry—so sorry,' he said with concern, 'but I thought you'd say no. I really did think you'd say no, and then tell me to go jump in a lake.'

'Or the Tweed.' She laughed, remembering.

'Lord, yes.' He chuckled. 'I know I shouldn't have laughed at you that day, but you looked so adorable with all that water dripping off you.'

'That's your story,' she declared, aiming a mock punch at him, and saw him laugh.

Gently he took her into his arms again and ran his fingers through her short curls. 'You know, it feels so strange to do that after it having been so long,' he observed.

'It's awful, isn't it?' she sighed into his neck. 'As soon as I'd done it I knew it was a mistake.'

'Why did you decide to get it cut in the first place?' he asked curiously.

A deep flush of colour crept over her cheeks. 'To get back at you. You see, my hair was the one thing—the only thing—you ever raved about,' she continued hurriedly as a deep frown appeared on his forehead, 'and I thought if I got it all cut off it would show you that I didn't give a damn about you.'

'But, hinny, surely you know that I love *you*—all of you,' he protested. 'I couldn't love you less because you'd had your hair cut. I admit that I liked it long but if you want to keep it that way it's fine by me.'

'I'm not keeping it like this,' she said vehemently. 'I'm never setting foot in a hairdresser's again.'

'Oh, Isabella, you're an idiot sometimes but I do love you,' he said with a laugh.

'Do you?' she said softly.

'Uh-huh,' he murmured, planting a tender line of kisses across her forehead as though to prove it. 'In fact, I intend to spend the rest of my life immortalising you on canvas.'

'Surely not more pictures of me as the queen of the elves?' she said, smiling.

He shook his head as he transferred his attention to her throat. 'I've always wanted to move out of landscapes into nudes.'

She leaned against him for a second, enjoying the tender touch of his lips, then suddenly realised what he'd said.

'Nudes?' she squeaked. 'You mean you'd ask me…you want me to… Oh, Ben, I couldn't. Maybe if I lost a bit of weight, started going to a gym—'

'You'll do no such thing,' he declared. 'I like you exactly the way you are.'

'Ben, I'm too big and I'm too fat,' she said bluntly.

'You're not. You're all womanly curves and I love every inch of you.'

Her face softened. 'Do you?'

He nodded. 'And I intend to paint you dozens of times to prove it.'

His lips captured hers and for a second she surrendered to them, only to pull herself free abruptly.

'Just a minute,' she said breathlessly. 'Where do you intend putting all these paintings of me?'

'The sitting room, the dining room, the hall—'

'No way—absolutely not,' she gasped. 'I'm not having visitors staring at pictures of me with no clothes on.'

He sighed as he drew her back into his arms. 'OK, we'll just have one big painting of you over our bed.'

'But that would be as bad as having a mirror on the ceiling,' she protested.

A smile tugged at the corner of his lips. 'A mirror on the ceiling? I like the sound of that.'

'Ben Farrell, if you think I'm going to allow you to put—'

'We'll discuss it after we're married,' he interrupted, beginning to kiss her again.

'No, we won't. Ben, I was only joking about the mirr—'

'Izzie.'

'What?'

'This is becoming demoralising,' he said. 'I'm trying to make passionate love to you, and you keep talking.'

'I know but, Ben—'

'Isabella, shut up.'

'What?' she cried, incensed.

'Hinny, shut up.'

And as his mouth claimed hers with a passion that took her breath away she did.

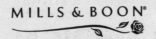

MILLS & BOON®

Makes any time special

Enjoy a romantic novel from
Mills & Boon®

Presents...™   *Enchanted*™   *Temptation*®

Historical Romance™   *Medical Romance*™

MILLS & BOON®

MEDICAL ROMANCE™

HER PASSION FOR DR JONES by Lilian Darcy
Southshore - No.1 of 4

Dr Harry Jones is sure it's a mistake having Rebecca Irwin work in the practice. Despite the raging attraction between her and Harry, Rebecca fought her corner!

BACHELOR CURE by Marion Lennox
Bachelor Doctors

Dr Tessa Westcott burst into Mike Llewellyn's life like a red-headed whirlwind. She said exactly what she thought, and turned his ordered world upside down. It couldn't last. But Mike had to admit, she lightened his life.

HOLDING THE BABY by Laura MacDonald

Lewis's sister was abroad and he was left holding the baby—literally! He *badly* needed help with the three children and asked Jo Henry to be nanny. In a family situation, Jo and Lewis became *vividly* aware of each other...

SEVENTH DAUGHTER by Gill Sanderson

Specialist registrar Dr James Owen was everything Dr Delyth Price ever wanted in a man. But Delyth had a gift not everyone understood. James seemed prepared to listen, if not to believe. Then she discovered his lighthearted side, and fell even deeper into love...

Available from 3rd September 1999

MILLS & BOON®

Next Month's Romance Titles

♡

Each month you can choose from a wide variety of romance novels from Mills & Boon®. Below are the new titles to look out for next month from the Presents...™ and Enchanted™ series.

Presents...™

Enchanted™

On sale from 3rd September 1999

H1 9908

Available at most branches of WH Smith, Tesco, Asda, Martins, Borders, Easons, Volume One/James Thin and most good paperback bookshops

FREE!

2 Books
and a surprise gift!

We would like to take this opportunity to thank you for reading this Mills & Boon® book by offering you the chance to take TWO more specially selected titles from the Medical Romance™ series absolutely FREE! We're also making this offer to introduce you to the benefits of the Reader Service™—

- ★ FREE home delivery
- ★ FREE gifts and competitions
- ★ FREE monthly Newsletter
- ★ Books available before they're in the shops
- ★ Exclusive Reader Service discounts

Accepting these FREE books and gift places you under no obligation to buy; you may cancel at any time, even after receiving your free shipment. Simply complete your details below and return the entire page to the address below. **You don't even need a stamp!**

YES! Please send me 2 free Medical Romance books and a surprise gift. I understand that unless you hear from me, I will receive 4 superb new titles every month for just £2.40 each, postage and packing free. I am under no obligation to purchase any books and may cancel my subscription at any time. The free books and gift will be mine to keep in any case.

M9EB

Ms/Mrs/Miss/Mr ....Initials...
BLOCK CAPITALS PLEASE

Surname...

Address...

....Postcode ....

Send this whole page to:
THE READER SERVICE, FREEPOST CN81, CROYDON, CR9 3WZ
(Eire readers please send coupon to: P.O. BOX 4546, KILCOCK, COUNTY KILDARE)

Spoil yourself next month
with these four novels from

TEMPTATION

MACKENZIE'S WOMAN by JoAnn Ross

Bachelor Auction

Kate Campbell had to persuade Alec Mackenzie to take part in a
charity bachelor auction. This rugged adventurer would have
women bidding millions for an hour of his time. Trouble was,
Alec wasn't really a bachelor. Though nobody knew it—he was
married to Kate!

A PRIVATE EYEFUL by Ruth Jean Dale

Hero for Hire

Nick Charles was a bodyguard on a vital assignment. But no one
had yet told him exactly what that assignment was! So he was
hanging around a luxury resort, waiting… Then along came
luscious Cory Leblanc and Nick just knew she was a prime
candidate—for *something*…

PRIVATE LESSONS by Julie Elizabeth Leto

Blaze

'Harley' turned up on Grant Riordan's doorstep and sent his
libido skyrocketing. Hired as the 'entertainment' for a bachelor
party, she was dressed like an exotic dancer but had the eyes of
an innocent. Unfortunately, after a little accident, she didn't
have a clue who she was…

SEDUCING SYDNEY by Kathy Marks

Plain-Jane Sydney Stone was feeling seriously out of place in a
glamorous Las Vegas hotel, when she received a mysterious
note arranging a date—for that night! She was sure the message
must have been delivered to the wrong woman. But maybe
she'd just go and find out…

9908